FROM CAFÉS TO COSSACKS

The Time Orb Series Book III

CALLIE BERKHAM

All rights reserved. No part of this book may be reproduced or transmitted in any form or by any means, electronic or mechanical, including photocopying, recording, or by any information storage and retrieval system, without permission in writing from the publisher.
From Cafés to Cossacks:
The Time Orb Series Book III
Published in 2020 by DCF Books
Cover design by Gabrielle Prendergast

 A catalogue record for this book is available from the National Library of Australia

ISBN: 978-0-9945011-5-8
Also available in eBook
ISBN: 978-0-9945011-4-1 (ebk)
Copyright © Callie Berkham 2020

This book is a work of fiction and all characters and events are fictitious. Any resemblance to real persons, living or dead, or any events past or present are purely coincidental.

CHAPTER 1

Max sat gazing out over the grounds, the mountains in the distance ringed by early morning fog. She couldn't think of a nicer place to be at that moment.

They had been home for nearly a month, and Max still couldn't stop thinking about her sisters. First Abby fell for the very hunky laird, and then Izzy succumbed to the charms of the handsome earl.

Not only had they fallen in love with their men, but they fell in love with the times they found themselves in. Max combed her dark hair back with her fingers and let out a laugh. Trying to figure out how they could give up present-day conveniences made her head hurt.

Abby especially. At least Izzy had some comforts, the Earl's money and title assured that, but Abby? The castle was drafty, the food was simple, and the clothes, goodness—fashionable Abby, who used to spend much of her free time being pampered in day spas when she wasn't traipsing around the world giving historical lectures to eager young minds. Even then, she would seek out beauty parlors and had found many in places like Egypt and Turkey.

Max would never have believed 1746 could possibly keep her sophisticated elder sister content. For Pete's sake, Abby didn't have electricity, heating except for great wooden fireplaces, and no running water. They didn't even have a proper sanitization system, although Abby said she would change that as soon as she could. But, Max had to admit, Abby was not only content but deliriously happy. So too was her little sister, Izzy.

Max made her way to the stables. The hairs on the back of her neck stood up, making her skin tingle. She turned around. Bree stood at the library window. Max frowned. She couldn't see her cousin's eyes, but by the way she held her head, chin pointed down and her finger tapping her jawline, Max had the distinct feeling she was contemplating something.

Bree turned away from the window and retreated into the room. Max shrugged and hurried to the stable. Her cousin was impossible to read anyway.

Garrett had already saddled both horses and had mounted his bay gelding. Max trailed her hands over Charlie's legs just to make sure there were no sore spots.

"I already checked him," Garrett said, glaring down at her.

"Sorry." She grimaced and then did the same with her own horse.

"And I checked Star too."

"Well, two checks are better than one."

Garrett harrumphed but didn't say any more on the matter.

Max swung up onto her gelding, Midnight Star, so called because he was black except for the white star on his forehead. Garrett's horse was a bay quarter horse with black mane and tail. Charlie was beautiful and faster than any horse on the property over a short distance, but Star was part thoroughbred. While leaner, he had a big heart and could gallop all day long.

"Hey," Max said, patting Star's neck. "Thanks for this."

"No problem. Let's walk for a bit, warm them up."

They rounded the back of the stables and walked side by side through the trees toward the Cascade Mountains.

Max glanced at her brother. "So why the early ride?"

"I didn't want Bree to overhear our conversation."

"Good thinking. She's acting really strange lately, and I keep getting the feeling she's hiding something from us."

"Yeah, I do too." Garrett moved his horse closer to Star. "And I'm positive it has something to do with the time device. I'm half-convinced we should lock it up and never let anyone near it again, but I keep thinking, what if Abs or Izzy wants to come home?"

"Exactly. We have to check in with them from time to time. Remember, we all Mom and Dad wants us all to use it to travel to the past at least once. I've thought long and hard about this, Garrett, and I want a chance to go somewhere."

"No. I'll go next. Maybe things will work as they should this time, and I'll come back when I'm supposed to—in one piece. Once I know it's working properly, I won't worry so much when you go."

Max couldn't believe he was acting like it was his decision. She was older than him, and as such, she held higher authority. Just because he was a man didn't mean he could tell her what to do.

"Uh-huh. I'm going next."

He directed a hard gaze in her direction. "No. I am, Maxine."

Max huffed.

Once they were out of the trees, they climbed a small hill overlooking the open field stretching onward to the mountains. In the distance, the huge old bristlecone pine tree stood alone. It heralded the end of the Davis's property and was everyone's favorite tree.

"I'll race you to our tree for it, then." With that, Max heeled Star's sides and pushed her horse forward. "Go, Star!"

"Cheat," Garrett yelled from behind.

Max soon heard his horse's galloping hooves closing in on her. She urged Star to go faster, and her frisky gelding kicked up his hind legs, making Max cry out in delight.

That little stutter had Garrett gaining enough distance to reach her side.

Max laughed and urged Star on as they flew over the grass. She knew she could never win a fair race with Garrett, but she'd hoped that taking him by surprise would let Star keep the lead. She was still half a body length in front. She urged him on. "Go Star baby, go!"

They were nearly at the bristlecone pine tree when Garrett cursed behind her. He hit the ground with a dull thump and a grunt. She pulled Star up and spun back as Charlie trotted past. Max leapt off her horse and raced back to Garrett.

"What happened? Are you all right?"

He nodded, clutching his waist with one hand while holding the other hand out, palm up. She waited. He needed to get his breath, but his leg had twisted under him.

"Let me pull your leg out."

Garrett moaned. "No. Don't."

"Fine." Max backed off and seeing Charlie nibbling grass nearby, she hurried to the horse and checked he was all right.

Finally, Garrett sat up. He straightened his leg with a curse. "I think I broke my ankle."

"What happened?" Max asked. Garrett never lost his seat. He was the best rider Max had ever known.

"Something spooked him."

Max scanned the ground. "Did you see anything?"

"Nah, probably just a rabbit or some such."

"I hope it wasn't a snake."

Garrett made a rattle noise, like he was rapidly playing a castanet, and Max hit him. "Stop that, you know I hate that sound."

"Why do you think I do it?" He made the noise again and laughed.

When Max was eight years old, a rattler had bitten her lower leg while she was hiking with her sisters and cousin. She still had nightmares about it. She was lucky because the snake's teeth hadn't penetrated her boot, but the sound of a rattlesnake was still enough to send her heart racing and cover her face in a clammy sweat. Garrett knew that, and he still tried to scare her all the time.

"Fine, you can stay here then. I'm going home."

"Stop being a baby and help me onto Charlie."

Once Garrett was back in the saddle, he grinned at Max. "You know, if you're going to be a vet, you're going to have to treat snakes, right? People have them for pets nowadays."

"If I decide to go down that road, I'll only specialize in large animals."

"You might not have a choice. There's probably some sort of Hippocratic Oath for vets that you have to treat all animals if they are hurt."

Max frowned. She hadn't heard of anything like that but hoped Garrett was wrong.

Garrett chuckled as he urged Charlie back to the stables.

A trip to the hospital had confirmed that Garrett's ankle was broken, and now back at the family home, he grunted, cursed, and moaned about having to use crutches to get about. Not wanting to learn how to navigate stairs, he decided to set up a bed in the study.

Max helped by dragging a trundle bed up from the basement. Once the bed was made, she sat down. "You can't go anywhere with that thing." She pointed at the white cast on his foot. "Especially back in time. It's too dangerous. I would have won the race anyway, so I go next."

He gave Max a one-shoulder shrug and sat beside her. "Okay."

Max gaped at him. "Okay? Just like that?"

"You're right. I can't go, and while I was waiting for the X-ray results, I got to thinking. We might as well get the trips over and done with then we can get on with our lives knowing we did right by Mom and Dad, fulfilling their last wishes and all. And, Bree won't get off our back until we do."

Max swiped at his shoulder.

"You're right about Bree. She's definitely hiding something. She kept pushing, wanting to know how the accident happened and if I saw anything that might have spooked the horse. It was as if she was more worried about whatever the thing was that landed me in this cast than my injury."

Getting up, Max paced the room and stopped in front of Garrett. "Why don't we just ask her then?"

Garrett laughed and picked up his crutches. "Why the hell don't we?"

Going first in case Garrett made a misstep on the stairs, Max slowed her pace as she descended the stair into the basement so her brother could keep up. She was glad she was going to do something, even if that "something" meant risking death by time-travelling.

She had been adrift for six months, not knowing what she

should do with her life. Since she was a small child, she had always wanted to join the armed forces. She hadn't cared which branch she joined, but once she researched the forces, the Marines instantly captured her interest. She enlisted and threw herself into training wholeheartedly. Bootcamp was supposed to be the hardest thing ever, but she loved every moment of her time in training. She worked hard to earn the right to become a Marine.

She had excelled in both the physical and theoretical studies, but sadly, her career had ended rather quickly.

Of course, punching a superior probably had something to do with that, even if she had been perfectly justified in doing so. Blast it, the beast tried to rape her. By the time her fellow Marines appeared, though, the only thing they witnessed was Maxine punching the daylights out of her sergeant major.

Unfortunately for Max, he was friends with the commander and the commander would hear none of what Max reported, so she had to endure a Bad Conduct Discharge. She grimaced at the memory. The court-marshal was a sham where Max's credibility and reputation were forever sullied. She doubted she could even get a job as night security now.

Maybe a trip to the past would give her an idea of what she could do in the present. She still wanted to protect her country, her people, but she couldn't decide what field would suit her.

Finally, back on level flooring, Garrett hopped to a chair and sat down.

Max strolled to where Bree sat on a stool at the long workbench. She was staring into space. Sometimes Max wondered what her cousin was thinking about. Maybe she was rerunning through life events; maybe she had worries and regrets like all humans.

Max glanced at Garrett. He raised an eyebrow as if to say, "Go on..." Max put her hand lightly on the woman's arm. "Bree?"

Bree flinched and blinked at her. "Max." She glanced at Garrett and seemed to come out of her daze. She stood up. "Garrett. How can I help you both?"

"We've decided Max should travel next," Garrett said. "But only if you can guarantee nothing will go wrong this time."

"It wasn't my fault Iz wanted to stay."

"Not exactly, no, but you're the one who encouraged her to go, not once, but twice." Garrett narrowed his eyes. "In fact, if I remember correctly, you were the one who urged Abby to put on that cloak, and you gave her the orb."

"So what?"

"It doesn't matter now," Max said. "They're both happy, and while we want to stay here in our present, we might as well do our parents' bidding as soon as possible."

Bree looked at both in turn, her gaze coming to rest on Max. "Where and when would you like to go?"

Max sucked her bottom lip. "I don't know."

Bree's eyes flickered. "Have you ever thought of visiting Russia?"

Max hadn't, but now that her cousin had suggested it, her heart beat a quick Cossack dance. "Ooh yeah, what about the time of the Enlightenment? Peter the Great's time." Max loved the idea of Peter taking Russia out of Medieval times and replacing long-held superstitions with science. "I'm not sure of the year. Hang on."

With that, Max raced into her room and scooped up the last journal she had been reading and flicked through the pages. Her parents had pictures of Peter the Great. Yes, there they were. Ah, 1699. Yes. Maybe she could meet with them there.

FROM CAFÉS TO COSSACKS

She hurried out the door, but quickly turned back and threw the journal on her bed. Bree didn't need to be reminded that Max's parents had gone to the same place and time. Something told her that Bree would find an excuse to avoid sending her to see her parents, something about the space-time continuum or some such rubbish.

Back in the basement, Max quickly said, "I want to go to 1699 Russia."

Bree smiled a thin, tight smile. For one horrible second, Max thought that she'd already figured out why she chose that time period, but Bree said, "Am I right in thinking the first of January?"

Max beamed and nodded.

She leafed through the green book, and Max wondered who her parents' contact was at that point in history.

"Why then, precisely?" Garrett asked.

Max turned to him. "That's when Peter changed the New Year celebrations from the first of September to the first of January in line with the Julian Calendar."

"Sounds fun," Garrett said, screwing up his nose. "When I go, I want to go somewhere exciting. Somewhere like the Wild West, or a pirate ship. You think you can do that?"

Bree angled her head and gazed at Garrett. "I'll give it some thought."

Max's excitement had her bouncing on the balls of her feet. "Where are the Russian clothes?"

Bree pointed to the costume room. "Ten rows back and to the left."

Max ran into the closet of historical clothing her parents had accumulated over their time travelling. She paused at the ancient Egyptian gowns and ran her fingers over the beaded neckpiece. *No.* She grinned. *Maybe next time.* She soon found the hangers she was looking for. She had to hurry. If she left her cousin alone too long, Bree might begin thinking her request over a little too carefully.

Max plucked down the warmest clothes she could find. She should easily fit in with the lower classes with the thick woolen socks and boots, the loose-fitting trousers, and the hemp shirt. She eyed the great woolen coat, hoping it would keep her warm enough.

Garrett laughed when she walked out. "Why are you dressed like a boy?"

"With my short hair and no makeup, I should pass for a guy, albeit a pretty one. I think it would be safer than being a girl in those times."

"She's right," Bree said. "It will be safer."

"Well you won't be there long enough to be hurt as a girl or a boy," Garrett said, standing up with his crutches under his arms. "We'll give you eight hours and that's all, right, Bree?"

"Eight hours?" Max said, her eyes narrowing at Garrett. "You want me to go back all that way and not even stay for an entire day? No. I want two days minimum, preferably more." She held out her arm. "Bree, set that thing and give it to me."

"Fine," Garrett said. "But I'm pulling you back here in exactly two days."

Max lifted her chin and glared at him. She didn't have time to argue. "Fine."

She hid her smile as she took the orb. Two days would probably be enough, but if she connected with their parents and was having a good time, she'd screw with the orb until she was good and ready to return.

Bree nodded, set the orb to the coordinates, and held it out to Max. "Your contact is Ilya Kutepov. You should arrive close to his whereabouts but if you don't connect immediately, just ask someone where you can find him. He's well known in the region."

Garrett grabbed Max's arm.

Max spun toward him, and her nose almost touched the bottom of his neck. She instinctively twisted and broke out of his grasp.

"Maxine," Garrett's voice broke through her focus. She had to stop her leg from coming up to knee him. Instead, she stepped back and let her hands hang by her sides.

"Garrett, you know not to sneak up on me like that."

"Sorry." He dropped the corners of his mouth and made a puppy-dog face. "I just wanted to give you a goodbye hug."

Max laughed and wrapped her arms around him. "Thank you, little brother."

Garrett pulled her in tight. "Please come back."

Giving him a final squeeze, Max answered, "I intend to."

She turned to Bree. She had to get going before Bree realized she was going back to the exact time and place where her parents would be. She had a hunch that Bree wouldn't allow that. "Let's go."

The moment she turned the top of the orb so the leaves aligned, its center sprang up and Max's body shifted and stretched around the device. It wasn't painful exactly, but the sensation was rather unsettling. She felt like she was in a cartoon, the ones where the character was sucked into a vacuum cleaner and poof, she was in. Or maybe it was a washing machine, because now her body was spiraling so tightly, she was sure her feet passed her eyes more than once. Then the pressure suddenly vanished, and she flew forward out of what she supposed was a time vortex. She landed, dizzy-headed, on the stony ground.

She stayed there with her cheek pressed against the thin grass, waiting for her head to catch up to the rest of her body. Animal noises sounded around her, and she sat up. No. Not animals. Humans pretending to be animals. Wolf howls echoed in her ears, but with her head still fuzzy, she couldn't make out the direction.

An answering call sounded not far to her left. One thing she knew, she had to get to cover. She repositioned the heavy coat on her back and scrambled on all fours toward a nearby shrub, but before she could hide, a hand grasped her arm and pulled her to a stop.

CHAPTER 2

Peter couldn't remember being so cold. Late Spring in Denmark meant sun, warmth, and colorful new growth, but in Russia, the cold still rested deep in his bones. The snow had begun to melt from the little sunlight that touched it, and the ground had turned into mud, wet and stinking.

His uncle had installed him in a small group of Whites nearly two months before. They had found refuge in an abandoned farmhouse a little south of Belgorod, but Ilya wouldn't let them light a fire until they were sure no Bolsheviks were close by. They hunkered down on the wooden crates, and Peter gazed into the empty fireplace.

His homeland had declared neutrality in the Great War that began in 1914, and the Danish king had sent a message urging Danes to refrain from commenting on or being involved in the war. Peter's being in Russia had nothing to do with the Great War, and his presence would be seen as family-related only. After all, his father was a Kuban Cossack and as such, Peter was also a Cossack by birth.

How Russia would emerge from the Great War and their

revolution wasn't for Peter to guess. He would rather be home in Denmark working in front of a warm fire than in a revolution. He could see both sides—the Russian royalty had lost their connection to the poor, and the politically ambitious used that disconnection to gain a growing following to oust the royalty and forge a new Russia.

However, many royalists remained and now they fought, dividing a country and her people. The Kuban Cossack Host, the administrative and military unit consisting of Kuban Cossacks, had joined the White Guard and fought alongside Russians and other Cossack units. Russia was fighting two wars—as well as the revolution, the Great War was advancing on their doorstep, and the people were being savaged by both. He wasn't sure how Russia would look after the revolution but hoped the people, especially the Cossacks, made a better United Russia after all was said and done.

First, they had to continue to contend with the advancing German forces.

Ilya, also a Kuban Cossack, and the leader of what was left of the White Regiment Peter had joined, shifted his crate closer to Peter. "Yegor and Vanya will be back soon. If all is well, we will build a fire and sleep in its warmth tonight."

"I am satisfied to endure as my comrades endure." Peter didn't want them thinking him a cushioned peer, unable to fight or live in this hostile country. He had to find his cousin and escape back to Denmark with her. That was his mission, and while he was sympathetic to the Whites' cause, he was only there to rescue his cousin.

"I am sure you are, comrade, but I know how the Danes enjoy their comforts."

Peter scowled at Ilya but kept his silence. It was no good getting into a fight with the man. He had his opinions, and nothing Peter could do or say would change them. The man didn't see Peter as a Cossack and from what Peter gathered,

Ilya viewed Peter's father as a traitor to the Kuban Cossacks because he married a Danish princess.

Even though Peter had saved Ilya's life in the last fight, Ilya never made mention of it, either alone or in the company of his men. Ilya didn't like Peter being there, and he hadn't tried to hide his feelings.

However, it worried Peter that the general of a regiment of Whites didn't appear to like anyone associated with royalty. He had seen White members change allegiances when it suited them. White one day, Red the next. Knowing that, he could never be completely sure who was trustworthy.

At that moment, Yegor and Vanya returned. "We can build that fire," Vanya said. "We are in White territory, so we should be safe from attack here."

A young soldier scurried to the fireplace. The troop had already collected enough wood and kindling to keep the fire burning for a day and a night.

Even with his greatcoat on, Yegor was skinny. Peter wondered how his spindly legs endured the weight of his clothes. Vanya, on the other hand, was a great, thick-legged man whose bear-like proportions towered over even Peter.

Yegor sat next to Kolya, Ilya's lieutenant. The man seemed to lack any distinguishing qualities; average height, average weight, average looks, even his hair was average brown.

"We did meet with General Antol Denikin," Yegor said to Ilya. "General Kornilov is in Belgorod waiting for you to join his army, and he had word that the Romanovs are to be moved."

"Where?" Ilya asked.

"He didn't say, but he expects his leaders to grow our volunteers as quickly as possible."

Ilya snorted. "We have already emptied the countryside."

He turned to Peter. "We need more volunteers and more allies."

"The Triple Entente has already come into play," Vanya said.

Peter raised his brows at that. Vanya always surprised him with his knowledge of politics and law, so much so that Peter wondered why he fought hand-to-hand. Surely, he would be more useful at headquarters, planning and strategizing.

"Ah yes. France will be with us then."

"Yes." Peter wondered how long King George would agree to the Anglo-Russian Entente. Russia, France, and the United Kingdom of Great Britain and Ireland signed it in 1907, but from what Peter had heard, Churchill was already making noises about the anti-Semitism burgeoning within the White army members. Thankfully, Ilya's orders came from a higher place, and all allies and volunteers were to be treated as friends of the "Russian crusaders," as they liked to call themselves.

Peter cast his gaze over Kolya. He had seen the lieutenant haranguing some Jewish travelers a few days past, so he guessed that Kolya was one of the men that Churchill had condemned. Ilya wasn't there at the time, so Peter didn't know how he felt about it all.

Peter didn't like fighting side by side with such men, but he had to gain their trust if he was ever going to free Karina from the hands of the Bolsheviks. At least he knew Yegor and Vanya were trustworthy. Both had tried to intervene on the Jews' behalf, but Kolya had ordered them both to stay back. Being the soldiers they were, they did as they were commanded.

Yegor warmed his hands, waving his long skinny fingers over the now glowing fire. "I don't think this fight will last long. The tsar has many allies, and he will not tolerate such treatment for long."

"*Da*," Vanya said. "We will soon be home with our families, back to tilling the frozen earth for our sustenance."

"You don't want to go back?" Peter asked.

"*Nyet*." Vanya smiled widely. "I want to find a rich woman to keep me warm at night and in comfort during the day."

Yegor laughed. "You have your sights set high, my friend."

"Not so. You can come with me to Petrograd when this is all over, and we will both find new lives."

Peter shook his head, but he smiled. The two men were close, and he hoped both found better lives, but he doubted that would happen. If this war continued, it would be unlikely that either of them would even survive.

❦

THAT NIGHT PETER'S DREAMS WERE AT FIRST FULL OF HOME and his work, perusing site plans, all pleasant dreams, but later, the dark of the night penetrated his sleepy thoughts. He and an army drove armored cars, forging their way into a town to rescue Karina. But as they passed through the streets, Peter realized the town was bereft of life. No people, not even a stray mutt in the streets. No lights in the houses or stores, only silence.

Glancing at his company, the driver, and two soldiers in the back of the car, he realized he didn't recognize them, and searching his memory, he hadn't even seen them in camp. No one said anything, they just stared out the windscreen in awe, until one of the soldiers in the back whispered, "I smell death."

Peter started and drew in a breath. The air was thick with cold, but he couldn't smell anything untoward. He peered at the driver. He couldn't have been more than twenty years old and his face was pale in the glow from the lights on the dashboard.

The driver stopped the car and pointed to the building ahead where the street ended in a tee junction. The radio beeped and the driver picked up the handpiece and listened. Putting the handpiece back in its cradle, he pierced Peter with haunted eyes. "Go."

Peter frowned. Was he to go in alone? He had only finished the thought when he heard boots stop alongside the car.

"Go," the driver said.

Looking out at the column of four waiting soldiers, Peter opened the door and stepped out.

They seemed to want him to take the lead so without a word, he began walking toward where Karina was supposed to be a prisoner. The house looked like any other in the street, small, A frame with two stories and cladded in wooden planks.

Sweat began forming along Peter's hairline as they neared the building. The street remained empty and no guards blocked their way.

Peter, with the soldiers close behind, stormed inside the building. It too was empty. The soldiers fanned out, searching every room on the ground floor while Peter, heart racing, waited in the foyer.

One by one, they returned shaking their heads. They gazed up the stairs but didn't move to ascend to the second floor. Peter climbed the stairs, his heart increasing in pace with every step. Sweat dripped from his hairline into his eyes, but he dared not wipe them for fear that shutting his eyes even for one second would be the death of him.

Once on the landing, the soldiers huddled behind him. He opened the first door. Empty. The second. The same. At the third and last door, he paused, took a deep breath, and flung the door open. Karina was there, prostrate on the floor.

"Karina," Peter cried.

He tried to go to her, but someone held his arms. He wrestled and squirmed, struggling to get out of their grasp.

"Peteor. Wake up, Peteor."

Peter gasped and opened his eyes. Vanya's big brown eyes were staring at him and once Peter stopped struggling, he eased his massive hands from Peter's arms.

"You were having a nightmare," Vanya said, straightening his back.

Peter wiped his brows. Karina wasn't dead; it was just a dream. He would find her and take her home and he would do it soon. "I was, thank you for waking me."

Thankful the nightmare faded from his memory, Peter had soup for breakfast.

Ilya told the men to pack up, but Peter said he would wait for Elena to return. She had gone to the village to scout around and see what she could learn.

"*Da*. Tell her we are to meet with the General Viktor Kornilov's army outside Belgorod. We will wait for you both there."

Peter stood up. "If you hear anything about my cousin, Princess Karina, please send word back."

"*Da*, I will."

Peter didn't like the glint that came into Kolya's eyes at the mention of his cousin. He'd seen the look before. After a battle near a village or farmstead, many men felt entitled to enjoy the spoils. He'd had to separate a Whites member from more than one peasant woman.

Kolya had met Karina before, at the house where his father worked as a gardener and knew her by name and form. He made it plain that he would do anything to get her into his hands. But Peter did not intend to let that happen. He had to find her first.

The man's giant hands wrapped around Max's upper arms, dragged her under the trees, and tied her hands and feet together with rope. Max tried to twist out of the binds, but it was no use—she was too exhausted from time traveling and her struggling only made them tighter.

He talked a lot while he gave her some dry biscuits to eat and water to drink, but she could understand very little of his broken English. She did learn his name was Andrei and that he was waiting for his ataman.

"You're a Cossack?" she asked.

"*Da*."

Max knew that meant yes, but he started rambling and she couldn't understand anything else he said.

The last thing she understood him say was "sleep." It was a command she found easy to obey. Time travelling had done her in, and she was beyond exhausted.

Max was awakened by the sound of loud snoring. She groaned inwardly, sure she had only just fallen asleep. She blinked in the surrounding light and peered at Andrei as the morning sunrays shone down on him through the tree canopy above. She wished she had a cloak to snuggle up in. He looked way warmer than she felt.

She sat up and tried again to break the ropes binding her hands, but just like every previous attempt, they wouldn't budge. If nothing else, Cossacks were great at tying knots.

Andrei sat bolt upright and Max, startled, gasped, and fell back against a tree trunk. It wasn't Max who woke him because she hadn't moved or made a sound, but something had spooked the man.

He looked around and rested his gaze on her, putting his finger against his mouth to keep her quiet.

She listened but couldn't hear anything. What had made him so wary? He got to his feet, but he kept his back bent so his head didn't rise above the bushes and crept through the foliage.

He stood up and spoke in Russian. An answering voice also spoke in Russian, but Max heard the delight in the second man's voice at seeing his comrade.

Andrei stepped back and made room for the other man, who was smaller than the Cossack. Instead of passing by him, the man grabbed Andrei in a great hug.

From his dress, Max guessed he was also a Cossack. His gaze found Max, and she gave him a nervous smile.

They spoke in short Russian phrases to one another, with the smaller man glancing curiously at Max from time to time.

He asked Andrei a clipped question. Andrei shrugged and said something quickly in Russian then spoke in broken English. He said he didn't know her, but he found her alone in the forest.

The man pierced Max with his gaze, and something flashed in his eyes. Max was certain it was recognition.

"Who are you?" he asked in perfect English.

"Maxine."

"Maxine Davis?"

Max's eyes widened and she nodded. "Yes, but how did you know?"

"I recognize you from your photographs. Your parents always carry pictures of you and your brother and sisters."

The only person in that time period who would know her, and her parents was their contact. "Ilya?"

"*Da*, that is me." He stepped forward and gave Max the same great hug. Pulling away, he said, "And this is my brother, Andrei. Andrei, untie Maxine."

Max smiled at Andrei as he undid the knots.

"Why are you here, Maxine? This is no place for a woman, especially..." He leaned forward and whispered into her ear, "...a woman out of time."

"I'm not supposed to be here," she whispered back.

"Ah, so the orb is broken?"

"I don't know, but if it's not, my cousin better have an explanation for sending me wherever it is she sent me. Where am I anyway?"

"Your cousin? Briana? Patricia's daughter?"

Max nodded, but she didn't have a chance to ask her question again because Andrei interrupted their conversation, speaking quickly in Russian.

"*Da*," Ilya said, taking Max's arm and leading her behind more shrubs. "You stay here."

Max wanted to argue but his tone made her stay silent and do as she was told.

Ilya and his brother crept around the bushes and stayed low to the ground.

After a moment, the sounds of wheels and the melodic fall of horse's hooves floated on the wind. As the noises drew closer, Ilya and his brother crouched down and waited. Once the last sounds of movement passed, Ilya stood up and spoke in Russian to Andrei again.

"*Da*."

Ilya joined Max. "We have to follow the caravan to see where it's going. You stay here, and I will send someone to bring you to me when I know it is safe."

Max frowned. Surely, her parents wouldn't have befriended a highwayman. "Why do you want to follow the caravan? Are you going to rob it?"

Ilya laughed. "*Nyet*. We only mean to see where they are going."

"I could come with you. My parents must have told you I know how to fight."

"They did, and I'm sure you are skilled, but for my peace of mind, I would like you to stay here. Will you? I will explain where you are when I see you again."

Max was out of her element, and who was she to argue with her parents' contact of that time? She nodded. "I'll wait, but I hope it's not too long. It's cold out here."

"You will be sitting by a fire before nightfall. I promise. Do you have a weapon?"

Max shook her head. "I didn't think I'd need one and anyway, I prefer to fight with my hands and feet."

He chuckled. "So I have heard. You will be safe here, but just in case." He handed her a knife.

Max pushed it into her belt while Ilya and his brother trudged away from her through the snow. "Be careful," Max called softly to their retreating backs.

"Da," both said together.

Peter was about to leave when Elena, Koyla's sister, finally came through the door. She went straight to the still burning fire. "The sun is shining, but ooh, I'm still so cold." She took off her ushanka hat, letting her damp brown hair down, and shook it loose. The lighter strands around her face took on a reddish hue in the light of the fire. She turned to Peter and batted her eyelashes. "Would you like to warm me?"

"We must meet Ilya and the company in Belgorod." He threw an extra coat at her, and she caught it in one hand.

"But I was hoping for some private time. I want to talk."

"There is nothing to talk about, Elena. I have told you I am not interested."

"You were interested enough that first night you joined our company. You held me like a small child."

"I was feverish, and I thought you to be an angel come to comfort me in my last moments on earth."

She smiled. "And I can still be that angel."

"*Nyet*. I am not feverish, and I have duties at home. I cannot afford a liaison here in this war."

"You have someone else?"

Peter thought about the woman his mother wanted him to marry. She was beautiful, in a way. He couldn't fault her fair complexion, her blue eyes, or her golden hair. She would make a fine countess. After all, she had been groomed for that purpose since her first breath.

Peter drew his brows together as he thought about the woman. He had seen her disdain and heard the condescending tone she used with the domestic staff more than once when she thought he wasn't looking. In all probability, she would only get worse as she got older. "Look to the mother to see what your beloved will become," as the saying went, and Violet's mother was a vain, selfish woman. No. He couldn't abide the thought of spending the rest of his life with someone like that.

Elena paced the room, waiting impatiently for his reply. "Well? Who is she?"

"My mother means to make a match with a high-born lady on my return."

She sashayed to his side and took his arm in hers, pressing her body against his. "You don't sound very happy about that."

Peter extricated himself from her hold. "I haven't made up my mind as to whom I shall marry, but marry I shall. It is my duty."

Elena harrumphed, replaced her hat on her head, grabbed the coat she had dropped on the crate, and made her way to the door.

Peter quelled the fire before following her out and, keeping to the trees, they made their way silently to the army camp. It must have been later than Peter realized because the sun was already setting. It would soon be dark, and they had some way to go yet. He picked up his pace, sure that Elena would keep up.

As they passed a group of shrubs, Peter thought he heard a sniffle. He stopped and listened. Elena didn't slow, her boots making squishing sounds in the mud. The noise wasn't loud, but in the growing darkness, every sound seemed exaggerated. Peter would have preferred absolute silence. Yegor and Vanya had said they were in White territory, but Peter knew the Reds were forever encroaching on areas they had previously thought safe. The Whites he travelled with thought the war would be over soon, but from what he'd witnessed, the Reds were gaining more territory every day. Soon, no place would be safe.

He squinted into the fading light. Elena was nowhere in sight. He inwardly shrugged. They were near the meeting place, and she had apparently decided his company wasn't enjoyable any longer.

A scuffle sounded under one of the bushes. He bent down and peered underneath the foliage. Something dark swept away from him. A black bear so far south?

A muffled noise floated to his ear. He thought it sounded like a sneeze. Someone trying to cover the sound with their hand? He knelt, uncaring if the mud soaked through his pants. A muffled cough sounded, and the bush shook as something—he frowned and corrected that to *someone*—clambered out the other side.

Peter leapt up and around the bush just in time to see a small form disappear into the trees. A boy. He took chase, but the boy was fast and sprightly, jumping low shrubs and rounding great trees with ease. Peter had the advantage though: his strides were longer, and he was able to jump higher shrubs that the boy had to circumnavigate. Peter gained on him with every step, and after some time, he bounded onto the lad's back and sent him to the ground with a great huff of expelled air.

Sooner than Peter would have expected, the boy regained his wind and struggled to be free. He bent his left leg and bucked with his hips so quickly that Peter lost hold of his right arm. He reached out to pin the arm down again, but the boy flipped over and knocked him back with his elbow. Twisting at lightning speed, he landed on top of Peter's chest with such force that the air whooshed out of Peter's lungs. While Peter was gasping for breath, the boy somehow used his legs to pin Peter's arms down by his sides. A knife's point tickled the side of his neck.

Peter stared at the face peering down at him. Short, coal-black hair hung down either side of a small, clear-skinned face. Large, sapphire eyes made even larger by the framing of perfectly formed brows stared at him. The forehead held tiny lines of concentration. Peter's gaze stalled on the full, pink, bow-shaped lips. Not a boy then.

CHAPTER 3

The small woman sat on Peter's chest, panting with exertion. The whole effect had Peter's mind going places it shouldn't. Her hot, out-of-breath look sent tingles shooting down his spine. He narrowed his eyes in annoyance. His cousin was the only woman he wanted in his life, not Elena and not this flustered woman.

She pushed the blade against his skin.

Blinking to regain control of his mind and body, Peter said in Russian, "Wait. I'm not going to hurt you."

She tilted her head in confusion. "Don't speak Russian, sorry."

Peter scoured through his memories for the accent. English, but not British English. "You are American?" he asked in English. When she raised her brows as if to say she might be, he repeated his sentence in English. "I'm not going to hurt you."

She let out a laugh. "You're not going to hurt me?" She stroked the point of the blade over his throat. "I'm quite prepared to hurt you."

He caught her gaze in his. "Do you want to?"

Her lips parted a little and sensuality flashed in her eyes, but the look was quickly replaced by confusion.

Peter chuckled. "I didn't think so. Could you let me up so we can make our introductions like civilized people?"

She narrowed her eyes at him as if trying to read his thoughts before letting out a huff of air and jumping onto her feet. She planted her feet in a ready fighting position, with the knife poised in front of her.

Peter stood up, holding his hands up in surrender. He gave her a hard stare. "I am Peter. And you are?"

The woman was still tense and ready to strike, and Peter wasn't sure she understood for a moment.

"Max," she said from deep in her throat.

"Why are you dressed as a lad?"

"I am a lad… a man."

He had to stop himself from laughing at her ridiculous attempt to deepen her voice.

"You are no man." He walked his gaze up her arm and, even though the thick coat hid all her attributes, his gaze slipped across her chest to prove his point. He pierced her with a look meant to intimidate her.

She tilted her head but never flinched from his gaze. "Obviously, I'm in disguise. What's your excuse?"

Peter had never heard an accent like hers before. She said she was American, but she didn't sound like any of the Americans he had spoken to. "Could you put the knife away?"

"No."

A branch behind her moved. Peter looked over her shoulder to where Elena had appeared.

"I'm not going to fall for that," the woman said, holding a steady gaze on Peter.

He shook his head to tell Elena not to strike.

Elena cleared her throat to let the woman know someone was indeed behind her.

Keeping the knife pointed at Peter, she turned to the side and glanced back. Looking away from Peter was a mistake, and her momentary lapse allowed Peter to grab the knife and twist it out of her grasp. He threw it to Elena and spun the woman around, intercepting her arm as she had brought it around to strike him.

With both arms imprisoned in his hands, he shook his head at her. "Don't try anything else."

Her arms were delicate under his touch.

"You can let go." Max's shoulders fell in defeat. "I have nowhere to go anyway."

He looked into her eyes, leaning into the cerulean pools, but pulled back with a huff. He prided himself on knowing when someone was lying, and he believed she was telling the truth. He let her go, but as soon as he did, she stepped back.

"What do you mean you have nowhere to go? Do you not live around here?"

"Ah, that'll be a no." She went silent as if in thought. A moment later, she shrugged. "So where am I anyway?"

"You are lost?"

"Yeah, you could say that. Don't worry, I know I'm in Russia. Uh, I was with a trading caravan but when I nipped out to... well, you know, they left without me. Probably should have told someone where I was, huh? So, what are you two doing alone in a forest?" She tapped her finger to her lips in thought. "Hmm, a Dane? In a Russian forest? And by the way you talk, an educated Dane." She glanced at Elena and grinned at Peter. "Who's your friend?"

She spoke so quickly, he had a hard time keeping up with her. He didn't know whether he should tell her who he was or what he was doing there. She could be a spy. He watched her face carefully as he spoke. "We are meeting the army."

"Army? What army?"

She said the words like she wasn't expecting him to

suggest they were at war. Everyone was wearing greatcoats, so she couldn't see any uniforms. "Did your caravan leader not tell you Russia is in a state of war?"

"Ah, no. He didn't."

Peter gazed at her. She took off her ushanka hat and shook out her ebony hair. It was only shoulder length, but it framed her face beautifully. He gave himself a mental slap. Why would a woman like her have an effect on him—surely, he wasn't that starved of female companionship? And if he was, Elena had made it obvious she was available. He frowned at the woman's hat. The wool looked new. There were no new hats to be bought as far as he knew.

She glanced around, once more looking lost, her large blue eyes like fresh snowmelt from the mountains in the soft sunlight. The top of her head only came up to his chin and her form was small, but there was no mistaking the womanly curves, especially the outline of her hips as she pulled her coat in tight around her. He remembered her full bottom when he lay on his back. She twisted her hair at the nape of her neck and pushed it under her hat.

"Well, thanks for chasing me down like an animal." She pulled her coat in closer. "I'll be going now."

She turned to go, but Peter grabbed her arm. "You cannot wander about on your own. It is not safe. You will come with me."

He thought if she was a spy after all, it would be best to keep her close. And, for some reason, he liked the idea of keeping her close. The last thought had him shooting an annoyed look at the woman.

She lifted her chin and smiled. That smile had sent his heart leaping into his throat. He had never seen anything as beautiful. As the sun's weakening rays caressed her face, her wide round eyes drew him in, and lustrous pink lips framed her perfect white teeth. He knew he was staring, but her looks disturbed his usual composure, and he could only stand there in silence.

She stepped away and raised her perfectly shaped, dark brows. "Lead the way, mine capitaine."

Her mocking voice roused him out of his fog. "Where are you from?"

"America."

"Yes, but where in America?"

"Ah, the West Coast."

He'd never been to the West Coast, and he didn't know of anyone from there. However, he was surprised they spoke so differently from their East Coast cousins.

"Perhaps you should contain your colloquialisms while we are with the Russians. They are a suspicious group, and a lost American would fuel their imaginations."

She winked at him. "I can do that."

The corners of his lips twitched in a smile. The nymph had winked at him.

Elena made a small grunting noise. "Who is she?"

Elena spoke in Russian, so Peter answered likewise. "I don't know."

"You can't be thinking of taking her with us. She is probably a spy. Americans are not royalists."

"I agree, but it is better to have her near so we can keep an eye on her than have her traipsing around the countryside, meeting with who knows who and working against us."

"I don't like it."

"You don't have to like it; you just have to put up with it."

"Ah, excuse me," the American said. "Can you speak in English? I don't know Russian."

"Please accept my apology, we will try to speak English from now on. But you must realize Elena is Russian, so English is not easy for her."

"You're not English either, and you don't seem to have a problem."

"I spent some time at an English school. Why are you in Russia at this time?"

"I'm looking for someone."

"And who is this person you are looking for?"

"Ilya Kut-e-pov. I think that's how you pronounce it."

"Ilya?" Elena's eyes widened in surprise.

Max beamed at Elena. "You know him? That's fantastic. He said he would come back for me, but it'll be dark soon and I'd prefer not to hang out in the freezing snow. So, can you tell me where he is and how to get there?"

"You know Ilya Kutepov?" Peter wasn't sure if the woman was playing a ruse. Did she actually know Ilya, or was she just trying to find him? He would be on the Bolsheviks' most-wanted list, Peter was sure of it.

"Well yeah, I only met him today, but he knows me and my parents. Okay, I know you don't trust me, and there's no reason why you should, but he will vouch for me."

"It's a trap, Peter," Elena said. "She is a spy."

"I'm not a spy. Look, don't take me to him then. You go and tell Ilya Maxine Davis is waiting for him. See what he says."

Peter had thought she told him a false name, but she was at least partly truthful. "Your name is Maxine?"

"Max is obviously short for Maxine. So, are you going to tell Ilya about me?"

"Yes," Peter said. "We will find somewhere safe for you to stay while we speak to Ilya."

"Good." Maxine held out her arm to indicate they should go. "Let's go then."

Peter couldn't help chuckling at her speech. He nodded for Elena to take the lead. He didn't have to look to know Maxine was following because he could hear her soft footfalls.

She knew how to walk quietly, and he had a hunch she was used to stalking through forests. Whether it was because she hunted animals or humans, he didn't know, but he hoped it was the former.

He paused and waved his hand before him, indicating Maxine should go ahead. For some reason he didn't think she was a spy, but he would be stupid to take the chance.

MAX SHRUGGED. SO, HE DIDN'T TRUST HER THEN. THAT was fine by her, and she took her place between him and Elena as they walked out of the forest. She glanced back and he was staring at her, his face hardly visible between his woolen hat and upturned coat collar, but full of obvious annoyance. It seemed that was his permanent expression, or maybe it was just her who irritated him so. She focused on where she was putting her boots as she recalled his chuckling at her. Somewhere inside he must have had a sense of humor then, or perhaps he just liked seeing someone confused.

She decided he wasn't worth her thoughts and turned her mind to her whereabouts. She knew she was in Russia and by their uniforms, it could have been WW1, but she was sure they used horses during the First World War, and here they were slogging through the Russian countryside. She wished cavalrymen had found her. She would have preferred riding to walking. It was faster, for one thing.

Following Elena, who flipped her black cloak over her right shoulder as she rounded a crop of trees, Max didn't think the woman was too pleased that Peter had brought her along with them. The two had spoken in Russian, but she could tell they were arguing about her. Elena threw a hateful glance back at Max and Max smiled brightly.

She had learned long ago that a smile more than a glare

pushed people out of their comfort zone. It was her beaming smile that turned the sergeant major's smug face into a startled, confused one as she walked out of the military court with her head held high. She often wondered if he was still waiting for her to get her revenge. Just the thought that he was always looking behind, thinking she had some way of repaying him, made her smile even more.

They soon met up with three men, all wearing black cloaks and black boots, who Max guessed were part of their troop by the Cossack uniforms they wore. They were also on foot and Max figured they must not be far from their destination.

The men said *zdravstvuj* to one another, apparently happy about something by the animated tone of their voices. Peter and Elena both said *zdravstvuj* in turn. Then, one by one, the men noticed Max lingering behind Peter.

Peter followed their gazes. "Ah, this is Maxine. An American. She is lost, and I have put her under my protection."

He spoke in English, then added something in Russian that Max couldn't decipher. The men looked her up and down, some leering openly. She drew her coat around her, hoping to cover any womanly attributes.

"My Russian isn't so good," Peter said to Max. "So, these kind gentlemen have agreed to speak English when they can."

The men laughed at the word "gentlemen". They obviously didn't see themselves in that way.

Peter drew her close to his side, and the group of men surrounded them as they made their way through the thinning forest.

Max tried not to think about how warm Peter's body felt so close to hers, and she had to stop herself from snuggling in even closer. She didn't understand why he made her feel safe but decided it was because he had said she was under his protection. The other men then had to keep their distance.

Of course, Peter was a bit arrogant in thinking she needed his protection. He didn't know she had let him take the knife from her. She had been stuck, so the only thing to do was let him capture her.

She had only sat on his chest for a few seconds, but it had been long enough to catch his intriguingly earthy, masculine scent. His leadership, his scent, and she had to admit, his good looks, had her enjoying her first time-travel experience immensely.

But she wasn't there to smell Danes. She wanted to speak to Ilya, spend some time living in his time period, and then go home. First, she had to find out where she was. There hadn't been time to ask Ilya, but she knew without a doubt that she wasn't in the 1699, the time period she had asked Bree to send her to. There was obviously a war going on. She didn't know history as well as Abby, but she still thought it might be World War I. If they were close to the Eastern front, it more than likely was.

Max listened as they walked. The name Kharkov was mentioned, and Max was sure the city was in the Ukraine. So southern Russia then.

They talked about what was to come in the fighting. A tall, heavy-shouldered man said, "While the Romanovs and their retainers are held in Tobolsk, your cousin is not. Her caravan was attacked inside the White territories on the way to the Black Sea, and she is believed to have been taken to Kharkov. A small contingent of the Red Army guards are still there, but the Whites are taking over the city. They will not hold her there for long."

Max stumbled on a tree root at the mention of the Romanovs, but Peter caught her arm and held it until she regained her balance. She smiled a thank-you, and he took his hand away, with no return smile. His expression was unreadable, but she thought she saw a flash of anger. She gave a silent shrug. Whatever his problem was, she hoped he didn't mean to leave her out there all alone. She had to stay with them, and she had to make them want her to stay with them. She had to find out what time she was in, too. If the royal family was staying in Tobolsk, that meant it must be the latter part of 1917. *Good one, Bree. Way to get me in trouble sending me into the middle of a civil war.*

"Then we must be on our way," Peter said. "Does Ilya agree?"

A man appeared out of the trees. He greeted them in Russian, but Max recognized his voice. "Andrei," she said.

"You're here. Good. Come."

"Wait. Do you know her?" asked Peter.

Andrei then spoke in Russian.

They spoke for a bit, then Andrei trotted off back through the trees.

Peter stared at Max. She held his gaze, but when he didn't say anything, she thought maybe he expected her to speak first.

"What did he say?" she asked.

"He said you were a friend of his family."

"That's it?"

"Is there something more you would like to tell me?"

"No, no, it's fine. I just want to see Ilya, that's all."

He shot her a hard look but didn't say anything.

They walked in the direction Andrei had gone, and soon Max smelled burning wood and hot food. The aromas made her stomach grumble and she realized; she hadn't eaten since before she left her home.

CHAPTER 4

Bree eyed Garrett dozing on the sofa. She wished he would just leave the basement, leave her in peace. She wasn't sure she wanted him to know everything about the orbs, not until she was able to go back in time herself. They had all missed the little green light that was supposed to light up when the coordinates were set and the contact was close by. She'd been the one to set the coordinates for Abby and Izzy. None of them knew about the black orb then, and Garrett and Max didn't know about the date coordinates until Izzy found the book of contacts.

Abby was nowhere near her contact's location, but that was because the old laird had passed on. He was to tell his son about Mark and Dianne and hand over the position of being their contact in that time. But Iain either didn't listen to the old man, or the laird forgot, or maybe he'd thought he'd passed on the details to Iain who then became the contact without his knowledge. That was why Abby arrived in 1746 in the middle of a battle, a battle her contact was taking part in. That reminded Bree, she needed to update the blue book of names.

Izzy knew who her contact was before she left. Bree frowned. She was sure the light was on before Izzy left, but instead of Duke Chodstone, she met the Earl of Wellsneath. Bree wondered when Mark and Dianne had arranged the meeting. They would have known Chodstone had only just left that part of Fleet Street, and they would have known Edward would turn up there at the precise time Izzy landed in 1811.

Bree tried to remember if the light worked when Max left. She wasn't certain, and she silently slapped herself for that. In her hurry to get Max travelling, she forgot to check. She hoped the light was on—Max in Russia during the revolution would be dangerous without her contact.

She shook the black orb. *Work, dammit*.

"What are you doing?" Garrett asked, rubbing his eyes. "Don't break the stupid thing."

"I'm not going to break it, I just want to make sure it's working properly. Why don't you go to bed?"

He yawned. "Yeah, I'm beat. Wake me if anything happens and, in the meantime, don't break it, okay?"

Bree smiled. "I won't."

As soon as he disappeared up the stairs and she heard the door to the basement shut, she dropped the smile and frowned at the orb. "Why aren't you working?"

The answer nearly grew in her mind, but she pushed it aside. No. She wouldn't believe that for a moment. "He is alive," she whispered to the orb, her lips almost kissing the blackness of it.

She reentered Max's coordinates so the black orb could link with the white orb. A shiver ran down her spine as she placed the orb in its box. "Please be safe, Max."

After Mark and Dianne's accident, Bree was concerned with anybody using the time travel devices. It must have been hard for Carter to do what he had to do, to make it look like

Mark and Dianne had died in a car accident, but he did and until Bree could tell the siblings the truth of what really happened to their parents, it was up to her to keep their secret.

She sighed and dropped her head forward. She wished she could tell Garrett everything. She needed someone to confide in, but she had promised Dianne.

Bree's thoughts filled with the day she learned about the truth of Mark and Dianne's accident.

She was at home and had just finished feeding and getting the animals settled for the night when Dianne appeared out of nowhere. Of course, Bree wouldn't usually be alarmed by that. Dianne and Mark were always visiting her during their travels, always asking if she'd like to go with them again, but she never did, not after the first time. Bree hadn't felt comfortable travelling through time. It just never felt right.

However, what made that last visit different was not only that Dianne was alone, but Carter had told her only the day before that both of them were killed in a car accident. Her heart had ached all that day, and she found it difficult to imagine never seeing her aunt and uncle again.

But, there she was, Aunt Dianne, smiling like any other time she visited.

"How? What? Where's Mark?"

Questions spilled from Bree's lips, and all the while Bree wondered if she wasn't seeing an apparition.

She tentatively held out her hand to touch Dianne's face. "Are you real?"

Dianne took her hand and held it to her cheek. "I am real. I know, it's okay, I'm real. Carter told you, didn't he?"

Bree nodded.

"Come on, let's go inside and talk."

Bree nodded again and they walked to Bree's tiny house.

Once inside, Dianne sat down at the table and said, "I, we, need you to do something for us."

"I don't understand. How can you be here? You're dead. Sorry, that was a bit blunt, but well, you are."

"Not dead exactly." Dianne smashed her lips together. "Look, I know we're to blame for all this, but believe me when I say I'm sorry."

"What do you mean?"

She pushed her blonde hair from her face and gazed into Bree's eyes. "We're not dead, well not like normal people are dead anyway, but we were caught in a time vortex and have no idea when we will be pulled back. We arrived at Carter's this morning and while this is the longest time we've had out of the vortex, it'll never be long enough."

"Where's Mark?"

"He's with Carter—they're trying to figure out if and how we can return to normal time." She sucked in her cheek and screwed up her nose. "Carter isn't optimistic that will happen."

"So, you're both stuck in time, stuck in the time vortex." Bree shook her shoulders. "Yuck, I couldn't think of anything worse. But, how is it you're here? Have you come to let me know how to go back in time to see my father?"

"I had to take the risk that I'd have time to tell you what we need you to do. We do want you to go back to see Garlain, but first we need you to do something for us. You can say no, sweetie, but we're hoping you will say yes."

Bree ignored the tenderness in Dianne's expression and narrowed her eyes at her aunt. "What are you saying, what do you want me to do, and why aren't you talking to your children about all this?"

Dianne patted Bree's hand. "Because, my love, our children aren't ready, but they are who we want to talk to you about. We love them so much and having seen their futures, we only want to see them happy. Will you help?"

And that was that. Bree agreed to convince, coerce, do anything to make sure each of the Davis siblings traveled back in time to find their true loves. The orbs were scheduled, and each sibling had to go in turn. Abby first, then Izzy, Max and Garrett. Bree was to go back to her father's time once the Davises were all safe and secure in their new lives.

She let out a long, loud sigh. Max had to be okay; surely Mark and Dianne would have known if she wasn't.

But from what she and Carter could determine, Mark and Dianne's deaths were their mistake. Carter thought Mark had tried to turn them to another time while in the vortex. He should have known they had to return home before targeting another time, but he had gone on so many trips, had adjusted the orbs so many times, he must have thought they were invincible.

Bree's grandmother had always said he was an impulsive man, but he and Dianne had accepted the risks of time travel. They reveled in it with every trip they made, until that last one. Although Bree missed them deeply, she liked to think they weren't dead, but they were lost in time and she hoped they were happy wherever their adventures had taken them.

In the meantime, she had to see Max's future assured, and then turn her mind to Garrett and his adventure.

CHAPTER 5

Max and her captors soon emptied out into a clearing where a large army had made a camp.

The men were Cossacks, with their kaftans, knee-length collarless coats, with black waistcoats. Max especially liked the shashka swords fitted to their belts. They wore gray trousers tucked into black leather boots without heels, and some also wore black felt cloaks. She spotted a couple of men without the papakha, the large wool hats most were wearing. Bald except for a lock of hair sprouting from the top of their heads, she wondered if their heads were as cold as she thought they would be. She'd have definitely worn a hat if she had that haircut.

Hundreds of tents occupied the area and small fires were dotted here and there between the tents. Peter and his group made their way to a fire near the eastern edge of the camp. They passed a wagon and Max paused to look at it. The back was fitted out as a field kitchen. There was even a wood-fired oven. She hoped the mound of potatoes was going to be cooked, roasted preferably, and not made into vodka.

"Keep up," Peter growled.

A neigh floated over the camp and Max gazed in the sound's direction. Behind the stand of tents, hundreds of horses jostled to be the first to get the food bags some military personnel were fixing on their muzzles. Her heart leapt at the sight and she smiled. Ah, so calvary after all.

Shouts of greeting floated over the group, and their greetings yelled back in turn made the group's appearance something of a celebration. Max was glad to get to the fire and feel its warmth. Russia was darn cold.

Elena went straight for Ilya, who was spooning some sort of stew into his mouth as if he hadn't eaten for days. Of course, he might not have, Max had to admit. The woman spoke quickly in Russian and Ilya dropped his spoon in the plate and his hard gaze lingered on Max for a moment. She wondered if he was going to pretend, he didn't know her, but he smiled widely. He then raised his brows at Peter.

"*Zdravstvuj*, Ilya," Peter said.

Max had already gleaned the word was a form of greeting from when Peter and Elena had met up with the others of her escort. Ilya looked even more tired than he had earlier in the day, his eyes had black circles around them, and his mouth turned down as he spoke to Peter. She understood he had a great responsibility as leader to his troop, and she could tell the burden was wearing on him.

"*Zdravstvuj*, Maxine."

"Did you forget about me?"

"*Nyet*, I sent Andrei to find you, *da*?"

"Yeah, well this lot found me first. They think I'm a spy."

Ilya looked at the people surrounding him. "She isn't a spy, she is a friend of my family. Please, Maxine, sit with me."

"That may be true," Peter said. "But in these times, we can't be too careful. I would like to keep a close eye on her."

Elena snorted. "I am sure you would."

Ilya gave Peter a quick nod of his head. "She won't be here

long but, in the meantime, I am placing her in your protection."

Peter threw a glance at Max, but said, "She had become separated from her caravan. Perhaps we can find it and return her there."

Indicating with a wave of his hand for them all to sit, he shot Max a mischievous smile, and asked, "Tell me, how did you become separated from your caravan?"

Max set about telling him, repeating what she'd told Peter and hoping her story was the same. "But it was you I was looking for anyway, so it all turned out well in the end."

Ilya laughed. "It did indeed."

Max grinned.

The group went straight into discussing the war without any more thought of her. Except for Elena, who kept throwing Max hateful glances from her perch beside Ilya. Apparently, she saw herself as his right-hand man, ah, woman.

What parts of the conversation Max could understand had her admiring the passion and determination of the group. They believed in what they were fighting for and would risk their lives to keep the Bolsheviks from power. They worried for their country, and none there were afraid to voice their love for Russia. All of them included her in the conversation, even Ilya.

After giving their reports, most left the fire and with only a few remaining, Max slid closer to Ilya. "Can we talk?" She glanced at Elena. "In private?"

He eyed her for a moment then nodded. "Go," he said to the remaining people.

The soldiers left without an argument, but Elena and Peter stayed.

"You shouldn't be alone with her," Elena said, looking to Peter for backup.

"We won't be alone, you can watch from your tents."

Ilya took Max's hand and they left the fire and strolled around the camp.

"Is there something I should know?"

"Not really. I just wanted to talk to you without all those prying ears."

He put her arm through his. "It is good we have time to talk now. Are your parents well? And your sisters and brother, are they well? And you spoke of your cousin, is she well?"

Max wasn't sure if she should tell him about her parents, but she didn't want to keep anything from him. "My brother and sisters are, so too is my cousin, but—"

"No, stop there." He lowered his voice. "In my time, they are all alive and well."

Max beamed at him. "That's true. Right now, they could be anywhere. Even right here in Russia."

"I haven't seen them for some time. But I have hopes we will meet again."

Max hoped they would decide to visit Ilya while she was there.

"How long are you with us?"

"Not long, Garrett insisted I only stay for two days."

He laughed. "He was always the bully."

"He was... is still."

Ilya said, "Is there a specific reason you wanted to travel back to this time?"

Max gave him a wry look. "Like I said earlier, I'm not supposed to be here at this time, I asked Briana to send me back to 1699. She told me your name as my contact for that time period and I have no idea why she sent me here, but I think she did it on purpose."

Ilya looked as confused by Bree's actions as Max as he gazed over the fire, and although Max could only see his profile, she was certain he was processing his thoughts. And he must have thought of something because when he turned to face her again, his expression was no longer confused.

He smiled. "I am sure she had her reasons."

Max stopped and pulled away from him. "Hang on, you know something or at least you figured something out about why I'm here. Tell me."

He held his hand up as if to fend her off.

A soldier ran to his side, his weapon pointing at Max. He said something in Russian.

"*Nyet*," Ilya said. "Leave us be."

The soldier threw Max a warning look and backed off to his spot near one of the tents behind Ilya.

"They are somewhat overprotective of me," Ilya said. "Would you like some tea?"

"I'd like to know what you think about Bree and her actions."

"Truthfully, I do not know, but I can tell you this. Your parents told me once that Briana was their standby, that is, if something ever happened to them, she would do their bidding. I'm sure whatever she did was because of something your parents wanted for you." He looked around the camp. "I don't know what that is, but something, or perhaps, someone, here will change your life for the better." He wove her arm around his again, and they continued their walk. "Tell me about yourself. The last time we were together, looking at pictures of you and your siblings, your parents mentioned that there was a reason you were so sad in the photograph, but they left before telling me why."

Max wasn't sure she wanted to tell him anything; some things were best left buried. "First, how did you and my parents meet?"

He chuckled. "Ah, now that is a long story, and I will tell you all about it when we have more time. It's a shame you arrived in the middle of a war—I would have liked for you to have come to my village. You would have enjoyed staying with my family. However, I can tell you meeting your parents changed my life. I was mourning the loss of a loved one, one who I thought to marry."

Max squeezed his massive arm. "Oh, I'm sorry."

"*Nyet, nyet*, she didn't die, she left the village and went to America with my cousin."

"Oh," was all Max could think to say.

"I was angry and not fit company; I stayed in the forest alone with my sullen thoughts. I built a fire, but I found I had no strength to do anything else but sit there feeling sorry for myself." He gazed out over the horse enclosure. "I don't know how long I sat there, but I remember nights and days passing in a blur. I was alone and in such poor health I was ready to let the gods take me."

He shook his head as if he still couldn't believe what he was about to tell her. "When out of the air, two people appeared and stood before me. I was stunned, trying to make sense of what my eyes saw, but what my mind told me was impossible. I tried to swat them away with a stick, but they ran out of my reach and I was too slow and weary to follow them so I let the log fall and fell to my knees, saying something along the lines of, *'Take me then, Take me to the afterlife, I do not care.'* I cannot remember exactly what I said, but the woman put something in a mug of water and made me drink. I could not resist, so I did as she said. The taste was like nothing else I had ever tasted, but it didn't kill me. I slept then, waking every now and then to the woman, giving me more of her concoction.

"I soon grew stronger and started eating what they cooked. When I was once again coherent, they told me who they were and where they were from. Dianne also told me what she had been making me drink, it was vitamins and minerals. Magic, I would have called it, except they made me understand it was just science and while it wasn't known in my time, it was still just that—science, not magic."

He laughed. "I was what you call in your time a drama-filled teenager, and I soon became aware that my life didn't hinge on the feelings of a girl. My life was for me to forge so I and my family would be proud of the man I was to become.

"Your parents visited me off and on over the years and not only am I in their debt for saving my life, but I truly like them, and I knew I would like their children if I was ever to meet them." He turned to face Max, taking both her arms in his giant hands. "And I was right—I like you already." He sighed. "But this is not the time to visit. You can stay for a day or two but then I think it's best if you return home and have Briana find a way to send you back to me after the war has ended. It will be safer then and we will have time to get to know one another."

Max grinned. "I like you too, and I'm glad Mum and Dad found you before it was too late." She looked around the camp and sighed. "I think you're right. I should go, I could inadvertently change history if I stay."

"But first, tell me more about yourself."

Ilya had just shared his story with Max, so she felt she had to do the same. They stopped at the temporary fence and she told him all about her days in the Marines and how they came to an end. She also told how she was thinking of becoming a vet but wasn't sure if that was where her future lay.

"Ah, that is good. You have experience with horses?" Max nodded and he asked, "Perhaps you could check our horses before you leave."

Max looked out over the lines of horses. They all seemed sturdy enough, but some could be muscle sore, and she'd give anything to spend time with the animals. She smiled. "Now?"

"*Nyet*, it's getting late, tomorrow."

He gave her a long, hard look. "I believe it's time for you

to stop grieving your lost career as a Marine and stop living in the past." He chuckled. "By living in the past."

Max laughed. "Yeah, literally."

"As I said, you will be safe here for a couple of days, but once I have my orders, we will decamp and if you have not returned to your time by then, you must go."

Max smiled. "Thank you, Ilya. I hope I find out why Bree sent me here before that."

"She might have made a mistake."

"I doubt it, and anyway she agreed to me dressing up as male. It was like she knew exactly where I would end up and she gave me your name as a contact."

He smiled but his brows drew together in a worried frown.

Once they returned to the fire, Ilya poured a long draft of some clear liquid into his mug and raised it to Max. "I drink to you finding happiness in your future."

As if his toast signaled, they were finished talking privately, a few soldiers returned with steaming mugs of some liquid. Peter and Elena also returned, and Ilya waved at the man near the food wagon. Max hoped he meant for the cook to bring some food and coffee. She would absolutely kill for a coffee.

Again, the Romanovs were mentioned. Max figured it was late 1917 or early 1918. They spoke of the Romanovs as if they wouldn't be imprisoned for long. They really expected them to be freed and they expected the war to be a short one, one in which they would be the victors. Max knew, though, the Romanovs would be executed in less than a year and the soldiers' passion, their commitment to the fight, and the loss of many of their lives would all be for nothing. It was a lost cause.

She decided to soak up their camaraderie until they left, then she would return home with her memories. She wondered if being a Marine would have been like this. They joked and teased one another and sometimes even fought, but all the while Max understood each one would give their lives for his team. It was the very essence of team playing that she would have loved to be a part of with her Marine unit. She gave a small shake of her head. No. As Ilya said, she was there to forget her past and find something that would help her in her future.

The men handed mugs around and Max was overjoyed to smell the familiar aroma of coffee as a man poured the brown liquid into her mug.

She thanked the man and sat back to listen to her new friends' conversations.

While they spoke English, it was heavily accented and broken. Someone named Karina was in some sort of trouble, and Ilya mentioned Peter's cousin. It took a while for Max to realize Karina was Peter's cousin. She had been captured as she tried to flee Russia and was placed under house arrest along with many other royals.

She gathered Peter was there to rescue Karina and take her back to Denmark with him. Her chest tightened at the thought of him leaving so soon. She would have liked to get to know him more but of course, she had to leave too. She frowned into her cup. Family was the most important aspect in anyone's life. Maybe she could help Peter rescue his cousin before she left.

Max swallowed some of the strong coffee as Peter asked Ilya, "Have you any news where they are holding her?"

Ilya shook his head. "*Nyet*. But I have sent out scouts. They will find her whereabouts."

One of the other men they had met earlier said, "As I told you, Peter, we think the best place to head for is Kharkov. It is my belief that is where they will hold her before sending her to the prison camp in the White Sea."

"*Da*," Ilya said. "However, I will wait for the scouts' reports. I do not want to be heading northwest when east is our destination."

Peter said. "Thank you, Vanya, but I agree with Ilya. We will wait for confirmation as to her whereabouts."

He broke off some heavy bread and gave a piece to Max. She turned it over in her hands trying to see what it was. She thought it was some kind of potato bread.

"It's a potato and bran bread called r*zhevsky*," Peter said.

The bread was bland, but it was palatable, and Max dipped it into the potato stew and ate it thankfully.

After she handed her empty plate to the man who hovered around them, Vanya, the broad-shouldered bear, gave Max a cup of what she thought was water.

He drank his in one gulp, so she tipped her cup up and drank. The liquid burned her throat and as she coughed up her lungs, she couldn't believe the man had just given her a cup of vodka. He didn't even tell her to go easy. She caught her breath and glared at Vanya.

The oaf laughed and his friends joined in. She looked at Peter. He was holding back a laugh of his own.

"It's not funny." She put down the cup. "You could have warned me."

Peter held up another cup. "Perhaps you would prefer tea?"

She all but snatched it out of his hand. "Thank you."

Sipping it warily, she couldn't place the taste. "What is it?"

"Carrot tea, the cook makes it for us. It is good, yes?"

"Not bad." She drank the contents, but her throat still burned from the vodka although a warm glow was passing through her body.

She wondered for a moment if that glow was because of the alcohol she had just consumed or because Peter was looking at her as if he was drinking her in instead of his vodka. His eyes had darkened to storm-cloud gray, and he eyed her mouth while his lips formed a hard, thin line. That familiar look of annoyance filled his face.

He started and turned his attention to something Elena said to Ilya in Russian. Max decided she had imagined his look, and the alcohol was to blame for her inner warmth.

CHAPTER 6

Peter couldn't sleep that night. The image of Max and Ilya walking arm-in-arm, talking and laughing, had his mind awhirl. What exactly was Max to Ilya? She had said they had only met that day.

Peter awoke sore and feeling like he hardly slept a wink. He hadn't, at least not at first. His thoughts tumbled about Max and Ilya. For some reason, he couldn't, or perhaps his mind refused, to believe they were more than the friends Ilya had said they were. It just didn't sit well with Peter that they were romantically involved. Max had winked at him, and her beautiful smile warmed him through; surely, she wouldn't be so attentive to another man if she were to be married.

Vanya threw Peter's greatcoat on the foot of the cot. "Ilya wants to talk to us."

Setting about getting dressed, Peter eyed Vanya. He paced the small enclosure like a great caged bear. Peter knew from experience, the man wanted to talk about something that was troubling him.

"What is it, Vanya?" Peter asked in Russian. He wanted to

know what Vanya was thinking, and the man could more easily tell him in his own language.

Vanya plonked down on his cot, almost upsetting it as the front legs lifted off the ground then thumped back down on the dirt. In Russian, he said, "What are you going to do with the girl?"

"Who? Max?"

"Yes, Maxine, she could be spy. We must be careful not to allow her to hear Ilya's reports. She says she can't speak or understand Russian, but how can we know this for certain?"

Peter let his friend speak without interrupting. He knew his words were not his. "You sound like Elena."

Vanya stood up, his great bulk filling the small tent space. "In this instance, she speaks well."

"Ilya said himself, she is a friend but have no doubt, I'm not naïve. I have seen friends turn on friends in this war. I will watch her, and you are right, we will keep her away from any discussion on war strategies."

Seeming pleased with that, Vanya left.

Peter joined Ilya and his squadron eating breakfast. Max wasn't there. And while Peter was glad, he was also disappointed at not seeing her again that morning.

Ilya gave whatever was in his mouth a last chew and swallowed. "The scouts arrived early this morning. Karina is in Kharkov, but she is to be moved out within a month. No date has yet been announced and I believe it won't be. They will keep her movements secret. Once they have rested and eaten, the scouts will return to Kharkov. We will meet them again at Belgorod."

"When do we leave?" Peter asked.

Ilya held up his hand, took a drink, and then opened a letter. "Lieutenant General, Pyotr Krasnov, has sent out orders for all southern troops to make their way to Tsaritsyn by September. That's us, and while September is many months away, we will go there via Kharkov and once Karina is safe, we will continue to Tsaritsyn and clear the way for our lieutenant general."

Peter's shoulders lowered in relief. He hadn't even realized he'd tensed them during Ilya's report. He would save Karina and take her home to Denmark. His gaze went to the side of the closest tent. Max.

He didn't know how, but he knew that she would be where his senses led his gaze. A soldier called out behind her. Andrei. She turned and walked back to him. The coat she wore almost hid her body entirely, except it couldn't conceal the natural sway of her hips. Something pinged in Peter's chest at the sight of the too-friendly smile on Andrei's face as he spoke to her. She nodded and patted him on the shoulder. Even from that distance, Peter saw color rise in the soldier's cheeks and by the smile he gave Max, the man was clearly taken with her.

Max hurried to the campfire and after grabbing a small, tin bucket from the small table to the side, she scooped up some shchi and sat down next to Peter.

"Good morning, Maxine." He kept all emotion from his face as he spoke, but he noted Ilya's eyes were filled with amusement. He quickly averted his eyes. Had Ilya seen his irritation at Andrei talking to Max?

Peter felt out of his depth having two other men interested in the woman he wanted to learn more about. Women usually sought him out; he never had to worry about competitors. He continued talking to Max, "I hope you slept well."

"I did, thank you." She pointed above the camp. "What are those mountains called? They're so white."

"They are the Chalk Mountains," Ilya said. "And yes, they are made from chalk."

Max and Ilya's eyes met for a moment in some sort of private exchange. She grinned and said, "That's logical then."

Again, Peter wondered how she and Ilya could be so connected. From what they said, they only met the day before. Peter's brows drew together in thought. Just like his nearly asleep brain had conjured up the image of them walking arm-in-arm the night before, the same image lodged in his mind at that moment. Was their meeting prearranged? Had Ilya been expecting Maxine?

His throat closed at the thought. An arranged marriage, perhaps? He swallowed. He didn't know why, but something told him no. They were close but not that close, and who in their right minds would arrange for a marriage in the middle of a war?

Peter decided to keep an eye on the two of them. He didn't like not knowing the truth of their connection. He wondered then, should he just ask her? Of course, she could lie, and Peter wasn't the best at seeing a lie. His cloistered upbringing, the trustworthy people around him, hadn't prepared him for deceivers of the truth.

Again, Peter thought about how many White crusaders had changed allegiances to the Bolsheviks and vice versa. He eyed Ilya; could their own leader be thinking of changing sides? He scanned the group and looked out over the camp. Who there could he really trust with his cousin's security?

Max's appearance had unsettled him, and he decided she was the one to watch closely. There was too much at stake and Karina's safety was paramount.

Max tilted her head up at Peter and smiled. He immediately smiled back, then drew his brows together. Why couldn't he resist the woman?

※

ONCE SHE'D HAD ENOUGH TO EAT, MAX STOOD UP. "WANT me to check the horses now?"

"Why would she check the horses?" Elena said. "What does she know about such things?"

Max shook her head. "If you must know, I have some veterinary skills and I'm just going to check if they're healthy."

"The replacement veterinarian assigned to my cavalry regiment is delayed, so I asked Max to examine them before they are needed again," Ilya said, giving Elena a hard stare then smiling at Max. "Thank you. Andrei can accompany you."

Peter got to his feet. "I will go with her."

The corner of Ilya's mouth lifted in a slight smile. "Do you have a preference for company, Maxine?"

Max looked from Peter to Andrei, who hadn't moved from his perch or stopped eating, back to Peter again. "It's all right, Andrei, you stay and eat. Peter will make sure I don't steal any horses."

Andrei waved his crust of bread in the air. "*Da*."

Max tried to think of small talk as they walked to the horse enclosure, but she couldn't decide what might interest the Dane, so she asked what was really on her mind. "So you're only here to rescue your cousin? You're not here to fight for the Whites' cause?"

"Yes, I am here for Karina and no, Denmark has chosen neutrality in the Great War and that extends to Russia's internal problems."

"Do you think the Great War and the revolution are connected in some way?"

His brows drew together and as he rubbed his chin in thought, Max smashed her lips together. Why had she brought that up? Now he was thinking about a possible connection. She knew Lenin brokered a deal with Germany in 1917, but she wasn't sure when that was exactly. Some even suggested Lenin was a German agent. How else did he leave his exile in Switzerland, turn up in Russia and take the reins of the revolution, leading the Bolsheviks to victory?

She glanced at Peter, who seemed deep in thought. Why couldn't she just stick with asking about his cousin and not interrogate him on his personal politics? *Come on, Max, get your curiosity under control.*

Time to change the subject. "I might as well speak with the farrier."

Max hurried to where the horses were tied to a rope strung between pickets. Several men were filling nosebags with feed and placing them on the horses. Each bag had a number written on it and Max guessed every horse had its own nosebag. She asked the nearest man, "Do you speak English?"

"*Da*, a little. You are Maxine?" Max nodded and the man smiled. "Ilya say you come."

"Where should I start?"

He pointed to the horse tied to its own line apart from the other horses. "Horse not happy."

Max gazed down the line. The horse's eyes were dull, and its head hung listlessly. The soldier was right, the poor thing wasn't happy. She bent at the knees to check the sex. A boy. "Do you know what's wrong with him?"

"He lost soldier so is sad."

Max looked to Peter to help with the language.

"I think," Peter said, "he thinks the horse is sad because he lost his owner. Soldiers look after their horses and they bond, so he could be right."

"The poor thing. Let's check him out anyway."

Max paused. All the horses were about fifteen hands or more, but she guessed none were close to sixteen hands.

However, she could tell by their chests and hindquarters they were all well muscled. "What breed are these horses?"

"Kabarda. They are strong and sure footed."

"They're beautiful," she said, as she made her way to the gelding. He stood still while she stroked his neck. "I know you're sad, but is there something else wrong?"

"Horses can't talk," Peter said.

Max threw him a frown. "I know, but they understand more than you think, and anyway they like it when you talk to them."

Max smoothed her hand over his chest, back, stomach. The horse flinched but stood still. Max gently felt all over his stomach. When the horse didn't show any signs of distress, she increased the pressure. The horse sidestepped away from her.

She looked around the enclosure and couldn't see any manure. "I think he's got colic."

Peter frowned. "What can you do about it?"

"Don't you know how to care for horses? Surely you have some in Denmark."

"We do, but the stable master looks after their well-being, all we do is ride them."

"Well, colic's pretty common when a horse can't get to graze at will. They get hungry and scoff down their food when it's presented to them."

"Ah, so," Peter interrupted, "they get stomachaches."

"Exactly. Can you untie his rope for me?"

"Why?"

"He needs to walk until he dislodges the obstruction."

Peter untied the rope and handed it to Max. She cooed to the horse. "You have to walk, okay? I know it's painful, but it's the only way you will feel better."

Peter smiled. "You would make a good nurse."

Exaggerating a shiver, Max said, "No thank you. I much prefer animals to humans."

"You don't like people?"

Max fitted the halter. "Oh, there's some I love, like my family, but mostly..." She thought about her commander. "I find humans don't always say what they mean, and some are dark inside, so much so, they do awful things to other people."

She attached the lead rope and started walking the horse around the perimeter of the enclosure, glancing at Peter as she passed.

Lines had appeared on his forehead as if he was thinking hard about something. Had she struck a nerve? Did he know people who had darker sides as well?

Peter wondered at her words. He would like to know more about why she thought that way about most people. Had she been hurt in some way, so badly that she lost trust in people in general? He was curious, but now wasn't the time. She didn't know him, and she probably didn't trust him. In fact, if he was honest, she had every right not to trust him. After all, wasn't he hiding a dark side to himself at that very moment? Wasn't he silently questioning her honesty? He had questions about her and Ilya, but he really had no right to ask. He didn't know her, Ilya did, and even though he thought Peter's father was a traitor, Peter trusted the man with his life.

Max and the horse walked away from him, and he absent-mindedly watched the sway of her hips.

She said she loved her family, so Peter asked, "What of your family? Do you have brothers and sisters and are they like you?"

She walked the horse along the far boundary. "What do you mean, like me?"

"Animal lovers? Adventurers?"

Patting the horse's neck, Max encouraged the horse, "Come on, sweetie. You gotta keep walking."

Nearing Peter, her blue eyes caught his and he forgot his question.

"Yeah, we all love animals and I wouldn't have called any of us overly adventurous before, but I guess we all are." She let out a laugh. "Even my youngest sister has had her moments."

Peter pulled a feed bucket under the fence, upturned it, and sat down. "What did she do?"

"It doesn't matter," she threw over her shoulder as she walked away along the side boundary once more. "What about your family? Are they like you?"

"I can't say until I know what you think I'm like?"

"Oh, you know, arrogant, brave."

Peter's ire rose at her first word but sank into his stomach at the last. She thought him brave?

He plucked a stalk of grass out of the ground. "You think I'm arrogant?"

She laughed. "And brave, I said brave."

He couldn't help smiling at her as she turned toward him again. "Because I am to return my cousin to her family? I have no brothers or sisters, and Karina is my family. It is my duty to bring her safely home."

"Yeah, I'd die for my family too."

"I don't intend to die."

"I'm glad. But really? Do you think you have a chance of saving her?"

He frowned. "I do." But as he said the words, he wasn't sure any longer. He didn't know where Karina was and even if he found out her whereabouts, he didn't know how he was going to get her out.

Max continued walking in large circles with the horse. "For what it's worth, I'm sure you will save her."

He chuckled. "Thank you."

They both fell into silence as Max and the horse walked around and around. Peter was content to watch but became uncomfortable with sitting. He stood up the next time Max came past.

"Let me walk him for a while."

She beamed at him and his heart missed a beat at her exquisite features.

Handing the rope to him, she said, "You got it, Count."

He took the rope and kept the horse walking. "How do you know I'm a count?"

"Ilya told me."

"How do you know Ilya so well so soon? Didn't you say you only met him that day?"

Peter twisted his head around so he could see her as she sat down on the bucket.

She shrugged. "He's easy to know. Nice too."

They took turns leading the horse to keep him walking, while talking about Russia's weather and what it was like in their own home countries. But while Peter was more than happy to tell Max about his country, his chateau and his work, she seemed reluctant to go into detail about anything. When he asked her what she did in America, she just waved her hand and said, "This and that."

He loved hearing her talk, loved her use of idioms he hadn't heard before but could discern their meaning from the context of her words, and he was sorry when the horse finally emptied his stomach.

Walking through the camp, Peter watched Max covertly

with quick glances in her direction. Her eyes flitted in all directions as if she thought something would happen.

"So is summer coming?"

"It is, and the warmth will make the war effort much easier going."

She stared ahead, and said quietly, "It will indeed."

Although she tried to hide it, Peter could sense her discomfit. Her vulnerability was pronounced for a moment, but then she turned to him and smiled brightly. "I love a white Christmas, don't you?"

He returned her smile. "I do, and it is the thought of being home with family that keeps me going, keeps me intent on saving Karina."

CHAPTER 7

Max had been worried since her two day time limit had passed that Garrett would pull her back to the twenty first century, but nearly two weeks later, she was still there, spending time with Peter and helping with the horses.

Peter and Max regularly checked the horses, concentrating on the few who were used by the scouting soldiers. They were the only horses that worked. The veterinarian had finally arrived and the soldiers kept the remaining horses exercised by walking or riding them around and through the camp.

Max didn't think she and Peter were really much help. None of the horses lost condition over the weeks, and she guessed Ilya just wanted to keep her busy and give Peter some job that didn't require him cleaning guns or cooking. He was, after all, a count and related to the Russian royal family.

Peter didn't talk much and while Max tried to make small talk, he always seemed somewhere else. Oh, she knew he watched her, she had even caught him admiring her on occasion, but for the most part he kept to himself.

On the sixth day, Max was checking the hoof of one of the horses. The horse leaned on her heavily and she dropped his hoof and fell to the ground.

Peter chuckled. "That one is lazy."

"He sure is. Every time I check his hooves, he leans on me some but this time, he let his whole weight fall on me. I think he did it on purpose."

She held out her hand for Peter to help her up and at first, she thought he wasn't going to, but then he grabbed her hand and pulled her onto her feet inches in front of him. She gazed at his chest, noticing how expansive it was. She breathed in the scent of him, pine trees on a winter's day. Raising her gaze to his, a breath caught in her throat. His eyes darkened and his lips parted. She was held there as if frozen in place, waiting for him to kiss her, but his mouth tightened in a thin line and he let her hand go.

He picked up the lead rope of the lazy horse. "Do you want to continue with him?"

Max tried to swallow but her mouth had gone dry. "No," she croaked. "No," she said more forcefully. "He's fine and anyway he had his chance, if he has a stone bruise, he can put up with it."

Peter kept his distance from that moment and Max made sure she never fell again, but she decided if she did, she wouldn't ask for his help to get to her feet again.

※

MAX SLEPT WELL THAT NIGHT AND AWOKE REFRESHED AND ready for the day. She pulled on her coat and furry hat and smiled. It had been over two weeks since she'd arrived in ancient Russia and Garrett still hadn't pulled her back to her time. Maybe time passed differently, maybe it was only one day there. She shrugged and pulled on the small backpack

Ilya had given her, remembering her promise to Ilya that she would always carry the orb with her.

She stepped out of the tent. Clouds filled the sky that morning, but she noted a warmth in the air she hadn't felt before. Maybe Russia was in for a warm change.

Elena was already at the fire with Peter. Max wondered if the woman ever slept. She retired late, long after Max was asleep, and left early in the morning, before Max even awoke. Max grimaced. Elena didn't like her, but really? Evading her every day was getting tiresome.

And even though Max wasn't drawn to Elena's personality at all, she understood what it was like being a woman on her own and wondered why Elena hadn't thought of joining a regiment with female soldiers. Maybe if they went to Petrograd, she could find a woman's battalion to join. Max was pretty sure the Woman's Military Congress was held in Petrograd in the summer of 1917.

Max frowned. Of course, the fact that women fought alongside men didn't make the men see women any differently, and she guessed Elena knew that. Max felt that way a lot in her training, the men always making jokes at her expense, always jeering her and some openly wanting more than a fight partner. But she tried to keep it all in perspective. They were men after all, and they thought differently than women. While she saw things on an emotional level, she tried not to take it personally. After all, they also jeered and teased their own gender as much as they did her.

Thinking that way had Max wondering about Elena. Maybe she felt out of place, maybe she needed a friend, maybe Max could, well, maybe not be buddies with her, but at least find a common thread on which to build a better relationship.

FROM CAFÉS TO COSSACKS

Peter, Elena, and most of the men had finished when Max finally made her way to breakfast, except Andrei. He looked like he wasn't about to leave until all the food was gone.

"Hungry?" Max asked.

"*Da*, we move out soon and food rationed on march."

"We do?"

He stopped eating and swallowed. "*Da*."

He quickly emptied his plate and bowed to Max. "We speak soon."

Max smiled and nodded, but the moment he turned and walked away, her smile vanished. Andrei was usually always willing to give Max his time. What had she said?

After breakfast, Max made her way to the horses. She had enjoyed herself in the army camp more than she thought she would. She spent time with Ilya, at least as much as he was able to give her when he wasn't meeting with scouts or passing plastuns, which Max figured was another name for foot platoons. Or he was with his own men discussing war strategies and such.

Max didn't mind not being privy to their discussions—she preferred to spend her time getting to know the people and hanging out with the horses.

Peter caught up to her. "Good morning, you slept well?"

"Fine, I overslept a bit, all this clean Russian air makes a girl tired."

Peter gave her a quick smile and then as usual, went quiet.

༻✦༺

The next day, Max left the tent and stopped to turn her face up to the sky. She savored the early morning sunrays on her face. Having had hardly any sun on her skin since she arrived in Russia, she figured she needed the vitamin D.

"We move out tomorrow," Ilya said.

Max started and gaped at Ilya. "Tomorrow?"

"*Da*. Are the horses well?"

"Yes, Peter and I check them all every day. The colicky gelding is healthy again and from what I could tell, none were foot sore."

Ilya raised his brow. "Peteor has helped you every day?"

Max let out a laugh. "Not really, he doesn't know much about horses, but he followed me all around the paddock."

"That sounds more like the count. I soon learned he knew nothing of horses when he first came under my rule. I hoped at least he could help look after the animals, but he didn't even know how to check for muscle soreness, nor did he know how much grain to feed them."

Max got the feeling Ilya thought Peter was excess baggage. Without a defined role in the army, she could see how that could be. "Maybe he could help a bit now, I showed him how to examine the horses and I think he got a good handle on it all."

"Perhaps. Thank you for looking after the animals, but now you have to leave."

"But I only just got here."

"Didn't you say Garrett would pull you back to your present in two days? It has been over two weeks."

Max gazed without seeing over Ilya's shoulder. Her brother did say that. "Maybe he changed his mind."

"Hmmm. We do not have the time to find out—you must leave now."

"Please, can't I just hang with you for a few more days? I'm really enjoying being here and I'm learning a lot and... and the vet thinks I'm pretty much indispensable."

Ilya raised his brows at the last then shook his head. "*Nyet*, you cannot *hang* with me any longer. I cannot guarantee your safety. We could be overrun with Bolsheviks at any time."

"But I'll stay out of trouble and you said yourself, Peter needs a job if he's going to stay with you, so he and I can look after the horses."

Ilya thought about that. "The horses are important, but I could never endure it if you got hurt or worse, killed. Mark and Dianne would break their friendship with me, and I enjoy their company and their stories. No, I could not endure."

"I'm not going to get hurt, let alone killed. I'm not stupid, Ilya. I can fight if it comes down to it, but I've decided I prefer not to. So, let's make a deal: I'll leave the fighting to you and your army and you leave the horses to me."

He smashed his lips together in a thin line and Max thought he was going to say no.

"Please. I promise I'll keep the orb on me twenty-four seven and I'll leave the second a battle starts."

"Twenty-four seven? What is that?"

"It means twenty-four hours a day and seven days a week. It means all the time."

He let out a puff of cold smoky air. "I may live to regret it, but *da*, you can stay until we get to Kharkov only."

Max threw her arms around his neck and hugged him. "Thank you. Thank you."

He laughed and pushed her away. "I don't think it is me you want to spend more time with, it is Peteor, *da*?"

"I do want to have more time with you, but you're right, I'd like to get to know Peter more, and Andrei, and everyone really."

He pierced her with a look. "You will stay out of trouble and you will leave if and when I say, *da*?"

Max nodded. "I will."

Max wasn't sure what she was supposed to do, but she made her way to breakfast, past the line of vehicles, about seven armored cars and a small tank. They looked heavy and slow. With most of the troop on horseback, they would probably be faster than the vehicles.

※

JUST AS THE SUN WAS PEEKING OVER THE CHALK Mountains, the whole group set about deconstructing the camp and by noon, all was done. Peter joined Ilya by his car.

"Everything is ready."

"*Da*, and I'm glad you're here. I have found you a position in the army—you will look after the horses with Maxine."

Peter caught the smile before it appeared on his face. He'd been appointed to work with Max, and he liked the idea very much. "I can do that."

"*Da*." Ilya smiled. "Maxine told me she taught you many things yesterday."

"She did and I am thankful for her patience."

"*Da*," he said, walking away.

※

ONCE THEY WERE READY TO MOVE OUT, PETER FOUND A horse for Max. At a little over fourteen and a half hands, the gray mare was perfect. The mare—he didn't know her name—had decided she liked his black gelding and had wormed her way into Peter's heart after her rider lost his life in the last battle. Peter hadn't known the soldier, but he did know all soldiers looked after their horses better than they looked after themselves. The bonds grew, and in a battle, soldier and horse became one.

"She's beautiful and she's just the right height for me. What's her name?"

"I don't know. I didn't know her rider."

Max put her foot in the stirrup and mounted in one smooth leap. "Hmm, I'll just call her girl then." She patted the mare's neck.

The moment Peter sat in his saddle, Elena brought her horse alongside him. "We are to scout ahead. Perhaps it would be safer if Maxine stayed with Andrei."

Max gazed at Andrei adjusting his horse's girth as if asking his permission.

Andrei said, "She sits the horse well."

Peter looked then. She did. He hadn't even thought to ask if she rode. She might know how to treat the animals, but not every veterinarian rode horses. "You are also skilled in horsemanship?"

"I can keep up with you, if that's what's worrying you."

Max looked at Elena as she spoke, and Peter was impressed with her forthrightness.

Andrei held out a pistol. "Here, take this."

Max beamed. "A Mauser." But a frown instantly appeared on her forehead and she held her hand up. "It's okay. Thanks, Andrei, but I don't think I should carry any weapons. Ilya wouldn't like it."

Andrei tipped his head to the side and Peter could have sworn another silent communication passed between Max and Andrei, just like she was wont to do with Ilya. He wished then he could read minds.

"Is good." He put the Mauser back in his belt and leapt on his horse.

Elena narrowed her eyes but never said anything. Peter understood in a way—he didn't like how comfortable Andrei and Max seemed with one another either.

Vanya and Yegor took their places behind Peter.

They made their way down a muddy dirt road. Snow still covered much of the landscape on both sides of the road, rocky outcrops protruding into the sky every now and then. In another time, Peter would have enjoyed the ride and the vista around him, and especially Max beside him. Peter frowned at that moment though. Although they were in White territory, the Reds were increasingly intruding. No vegetation shielded them from any oncoming Reds.

"So, what's the plan?" Max asked.

Peter directed his gaze to Elena, who had moved her horse closer, no doubt so she could hear his answer. Of course, he could not tell Max the plan. Even if she wasn't a spy, knowing what they intended to do would put her in danger. The Reds were known to torture their prisoners for intel, and Peter's chest tightened at the thought of Max being subject to that kind of treatment.

"The only thing I can tell you is we are going to Donetsk first."

Three heads emerged from the apex of a small hill, their rifles glinting in the sunlight. "Take cover," Peter shouted.

Hauling on the reins, he turned his horse about and heeled its sides. Shots were fired and his horse lunged into a gallop immediately. A large rocky outcrop on the opposite side was his destination. Gunshots blasted around him and his heart leapt higher in his throat at each burst. His training in the military helped his mind to only dwell on the moment at hand. He glanced over his shoulder. Max was on his heels with Elena, Vanya and Yegor close behind.

Yegor's horse went down and, in a flash, Max turned her horse, reined in beside him and leapt to the ground. Peter yelled. "Get behind the hill."

Max, keeping her head down behind Yegor's horse, shouted, "Peter. Go."

Peter battled his need to see her safe and his need to stop the onslaught of the attack.

He swore and heeled his horse into a gallop and rounded the hill. Elena and Vanya were already scurrying up to the top on their stomachs. Peter dropped his reins and joined them. Guns aimed, they shot at the enemy, Peter trying to keep their attention away from Max and Yegor. However, he was hard pressed keeping his own attention away from them. He glanced at Max. She was busy examining first Yegor, then the horse.

He, along with Elena and Vanya, shot as fast as he could. Vanya reloaded his Mauser after five shots. The man liked the bolt action on the rifle while Peter preferred his Winchester M1895. With its lever action, he was able to fire at a rapid pace but in so doing, he emptied the box magazine just as quickly.

Elena said, "I think there's only one left."

She was right, Peter could only see one head left, but the rifle was turned and pointing at Max.

Peter shot a look to where Max was. She had pulled Yegor out from under his horse and shouted something at him. She helped him to mount her horse and he raced toward the enemy's hill before Peter could stop him.

A Red soldier ran at Max. She shot to her feet and waited for him. Peter couldn't shoot—Max was between him and the soldier. The soldier attacked and Max twisted her body, bending it to the right and kicking the soldier in the side of the head. He stopped but didn't lose his balance, and Max took advantage of his surprised stillness. She half turned and smashed her foot in his chest. He fell backwards with the impact and lay prostrate on the ground.

She quickly searched the soldier and seemingly satisfied he had no weapons, she pulled on the horse's reins. Peter was surprised when the horse stood up—he was certain the horse had been shot. The lone shooter fired at Max while she and the horse trotted in a zigzag line, to the outcrop.

All was quiet when Max fell onto her stomach beside Peter. "You think we got them all?"

Peter nodded his head. "I think so." And with that, he stood up and shot over the enemy's hill.

Max tugged on his trouser leg. "Are you mad?"

There was no answering shot and Peter let his shoulders fall in relief. How had the Reds known they would be riding that way? Yegor rode Max's mare from behind the hill, holding a rope that was tied to two Bolshevik prisoners.

Peter sat back down and eyed Max. She fought like no other he had ever seen. Where could she have learned to fight like that?

Elena scurried up the bank. "They're coming."

The main troop was riding their way, and Peter had no more time to think about Max's fighting skills nor to ask her about them.

He walked down and around the outcrop to wait for Ilya on the road, his thoughts filled with Max. She could fight, and she cared about her team. She was everything an army could want. Peter flattened his lips together. The way her exotic dark blue eyes flashed, and her beautiful face set with focus during hand-to-hand battle, and the powerful way she moved —she was a vision of beauty.

His brows came together in a frown. He had never seen fighting like that. She was different, like no one he had ever met before. He had to remind himself she could be a spy, but not one part of him believed that. Still, he couldn't deny she obviously had training. Her whole presence during the campaign screamed of her experience.

He glanced at her as she came toward him. She'd risked her life for Yegor. She didn't have to do that. Peter would have gone back for him, but she'd acted without thought to her own safety as if by pure instinct.

Elena, now on horseback, met Ilya as he approached. She spoke with him animatedly, pointing back to Peter and Max and then to Vanya, who led Peter and Yegor's horses toward them.

Peter wished he knew what Elena was saying. She would have reported on Max's abilities, but he wondered if she would tell Ilya about the woman's bravery.

Ilya sent a couple of men to the fallen soldier's location. "Tie him up and put him in car three."

His men nodded and left as Ilya reined his horse to a stop before Peter and his team. Yegor, riding Max's horse, led the two soldiers he'd caught close to Ilya.

"Take them to car three."

"*Da*," Yegor said, and giving the rope a tug went to do Ilya's bidding.

Ilya looked at Peter's group. "Glad you are all well."

His hardened gaze washed over Max. "You are unhurt?"

Max opened her mouth to answer but Elena interrupted, "Where were you trained?"

"I..." She glanced at Ilya, whose eyes danced with amusement.

Max straightened her back and glared at Elena. "I was a nurse in France in the war. We were close to the fighting and a friend taught us as much as he could between battles."

Ilya raised a brow at that but said, "Good." He narrowed his eyes at her. "We will talk when we are in a safer place." He turned to Peter. "They were waiting for you?"

"I'm not sure. I hope not. Perhaps they were scouting the road, and that of course means more would be camped somewhere close."

Ilya rubbed his growing beard and turned to his men. "Perhaps the prisoners can tell us."

He called out behind him. "Bring the tank to the front."

Max checked Yegor's horse again. The bullet had skimmed the horse's shoulder and although it wasn't too bad, it could become infected. The veterinarian needed to look at it as soon as possible.

"You'll have to ride with someone else," she told Yegor. "I'd like your horse treated and rested before continuing with his work."

"You ride with me," Vanya said.

"*Da*," Yegor said, and leapt up behind his friend. Thankfully, his robust steed could take the weight of the two men, but only because Yegor was such a lightweight.

Once they were on the move riding in formation behind the tank, Peter stayed close to Max and Elena stayed close to Peter. He wished Elena would go away—he wanted to talk to Max, wanted to know more about her time on the French battlefield.

But when Elena smiled at him, he felt bad for his thoughts. She was alone except for her brother who was Ilya's right-hand man, Kolya; a bear killed her mother in front of her when she was eight years old, and her father was killed ten years ago. From what Elena had said, her only brother had no time for her and while she had fitted in with himself, Vanya and Yegor, both Peter's friends liking her, something about her had worried Peter from the beginning. He didn't know what and now that Max had joined them, he had to admit, he didn't really care that much. Elena was close to Ilya and Peter had no right to question his general's decisions. It didn't matter anyway—he was there to rescue Karina, nothing else.

He turned to Max. "Are you staying with us?"

She glanced behind; a wave of worry washed over her face. "I might go as far as Kharkov with you but from there, I have to make my way home."

Peter didn't know why, but the way she spoke had him thinking she didn't sound very happy about going home. Wait. She knew they were to go to Kharkov? He was certain he didn't tell her their final destination; he had only told her they were heading to Donetsk first.

CHAPTER 8

"Oops." Max realized Peter had never told her where they were really going. Ilya told her before they shipped out. Darn. She glanced over her shoulder again, hoping Ilya wasn't as mad as she thought he was and didn't demand she return home so soon.

"How do you know where we are going?" Peter asked.

"Ilya told me."

"I doubt Ilya would tell you such confidential information. The soldiers don't even know our destination until we get there. That is how it is."

"Then how come you know? You're not even a soldier and you know all the plans. Maybe Ilya trusts me as much as he trusts you."

He didn't look like he believed her, but he couldn't very well accuse her of lying. Max was glad then that Elena made her presence known by moving her horse closer to Peter's.

Elena smiled at Max, although she wasn't sure what the smile meant because it didn't light her eyes, not even the slightest wrinkle in the corners.

"Yes, please stay with us," Elena said. "We will have need

for a nurse. I can help with injuries, but I have no real experience."

Max hoped her returning smile didn't look like the grimace she feared it would be and stared at the tank ahead. She couldn't believe she had said she was a nurse. At least she didn't tell them she was a doctor. She hoped no one was seriously injured because she wouldn't have a clue how to go about treating them, especially without modern medicines and equipment. She didn't even know what medicine was like in the early twentieth century. She hadn't started her field medicine training before she was cast out of her military career.

She gazed over the soldiers ahead and had to admit, she'd enjoyed the fight earlier. It had been a long time since she'd felt the rush of adrenaline, the singlemindedness of kicking straight and true, of not only surviving an attack, but being victorious. She loved the mixture of excitement and fear that coursed through her body in a fight, whether real or for practice, and wished she could spend more time there. But even if Ilya was okay with her staying with him until Kharkov, she couldn't stay any longer. She didn't want to be there when the war ended, when a new era began for Russia, and royalty was no longer. She looked at Peter. He appeared deep in thought and with his back rigid, she guessed whatever he was thinking about, it wasn't pleasant.

Maybe he was thinking about his cousin. She understood what family meant, and even though she was still mad at Bree for sending her to the wrong time period, Max would give her life to save her. She leaned forward and patted Girl's neck. Maybe she could help Peter save his cousin. Surely, that wouldn't be interfering in time. Even if she wasn't there, she knew without a doubt, Peter would have saved Karina.

As far as she knew, Ilya and Peter were to depart company at Kharkov, and what Ilya didn't know wouldn't hurt him.

Once Peter and his cousin were safely on their way to England, she would go back home. She couldn't get involved with the Whites' fight for freedom. It wasn't her fight and anyway, it was doomed to failure.

They made camp that night close to Kharkov and after Max endured a quick wash in the nearly frozen Udy River, she sat on the bank and watched the men take care of their horses. Although they knew she and Peter would be checking them for any signs of lameness, they still examined their horses from head to hoof and back again. Max smiled.

Peter plonked down beside her. "Are you well?"

"Yes, but a little cold. Does it ever get warm in Russia?"

He laughed. "Sometimes."

They sat in comfortable silence for a time. Peter gazed over the water in deep contemplation.

Max said quietly, "I'm sorry about your cousin."

"I will free her and take her back to Denmark."

"I'm sure you will. How is it that she was here in the first place?"

"Her mother was Russian and after she died, her father sent her here to be with her Russian family. He thought it would do her good, but I think I agree with my mother: he should have kept her with him. However, he was griefstricken at his wife's passing and I don't think he could deal with a child at that time."

"How awful for your cousin."

"I'm sure it was a bad time for all." He looked at her, his brown eyes full of emotion.

Max didn't know what to say so just nodded. "But why did Karina stay?"

"She was already living with her grandmother, the Grand Duchess Anericka. When war broke out, Anericka refused to leave Russia. She did, however, send Karina off to Denmark."

He let out a puff of air. "The party Karina traveled with was intercepted before she could get to the port."

"And I'm guessing she's in Kharkov?"

He eyed her for a second then said, "Yes."

"What happened to her grandmother?"

"She was placed under house arrest in St. Petersburg as far as we know."

"It was, ah, is, a terrible time for so many."

He eyed her with curiosity, but said, "It is."

Max was thankful he let her slip of tense slide, but his expression told her he didn't miss it. She had to be more careful when speaking even if whomever she was speaking to made her feel so comfortable, she forgot where and when she was.

Hoping to change the subject and get his mind onto more important matters, she said, "I'd like to help you free your cousin, if you'll have me."

He gazed deeply into her eyes and her breath hitched.

"I would like that, yes."

"Peteor!" Ilya's voice sounded over the noise of the camp.

"I have to go, but I will see you."

It wasn't a question from his lips, but his eyes were questioning. "I'll be there."

Once he was gone, Max went to the horses and checked them. She knew it wasn't really necessary anymore, not with the veterinarian and farrier doing their jobs, but she liked to think she was helping in some way. Once she was happy they were all sound, she fetched the first-aid kit from the vet and hurried to change Yegor's horse's dressing.

Max wasn't surprised to find Yegor there, giving his horse an extra handful of corn.

"When will he be fit to ride?" Yegor asked.

Taking off the old dressing, Max felt along the edge of the wound. "It's not a bad injury and doesn't affect his gait, but

I'm worried about infection. So maybe a couple more days." She pointed to the narrow end of the gash. "See? It's already beginning to heal there."

"*Da*. Thank you."

Max smiled at him. "I like how you and the rest of the men care for your horses. It tells me you are all good men."

"Not good, need horses."

"I know, but still, even people who use work horses don't always care for them as they should."

"How you say it? Stupid."

Max laughed. "*Da*, stupid."

Once she'd finished her work, and suddenly tired, Max made her way to the tent Vanya had said was hers, deciding to have an early night. Who knew what would happen the next day? They were at war, after all.

※

The next morning Max was up early and rushed to attend to the horses. She examined Yegor's horse and spoke to the vet. He was happy with the progress of the injury. He said a scab had closed over the cut and it was healing nicely.

She decided to walk the horse around the paddock and although she couldn't see any stiffness in his gait, Yegor still couldn't ride the animal, not until the vet gave him a clean bill of health anyway.

She spent the rest of the day helping to feed and water the horses, all the while wondering where Peter was. She decided not to go looking for him—if he wanted to be in her company, he knew where she was.

As she walked back through the camp that evening, she rummaged through her brain for any snippets of history she remembered. The Bolsheviks had begun moving into Kharkov, but still hadn't completely taken the city, so it must be before December 1917. She was sure that was when the Reds occupied the city.

Ilya's unit was to strengthen the Whites' forces. Max remembered the Bolsheviks did in fact take the city early in 1918, but the German army occupied the city by April 1918. She felt bad for the inhabitants of the city. War was their everyday life, until the Bolsheviks retook the city at the end of 1919.

Whatever the date was, Max couldn't help but think Bree meant for her to be there. Her stomach roiled at the thought that her cousin never had any intention of sending her to the time period she wanted to visit. The woman had to have an ulterior motive, her own agenda, but what that could be, Max had no idea. Ilya couldn't think of a reason either. But if Bree purposefully sent her to 1917, then it would follow that Abby and Izzy's time periods were also chosen for them. She dragged her fingers through her hair. Her head hurt thinking about it.

Max reached the tent just as Elena approached.

The woman stopped beside Max and tossed her bag into the tent, saying, "I didn't have the chance to tell you yesterday, but you fight well."

Max pulled her coat around her; the woman made her shiver with cold. "Thank you."

"More like a man than a woman."

Max couldn't stop her eyebrow lifting in question. Had Elena meant she wasn't feminine? "High praise indeed."

"That was not to praise you, that was to say you look and fight like a man. Peter likes his women womanly—soft, pliable. You are none of these things."

"It's war, Elena, and wars are genderless. No woman has the luxury of caring about her appearance when fighting for her life."

Her top lip rose in a slight sneer. "Peter and Ilya are aware of your fighting skills. They know you would be a good addition to the unit. Peter especially likes you for what you can do to help free his cousin." She straightened the soft white shirt she wore, leaving the top buttons undone. The effect, to show her full figure, was not lost on Max.

Elena threw her coat over her shoulder, her mouth stretched into that same cold smile. "Peter has asked you to help, has he not?" With that, she turned and sashayed away. Soldiers watched her pass, some openly leering, but none made a move toward her.

Max wondered at that; it couldn't have been easy being the only woman in an army full of male soldiers. Maybe having a brother who was the general's lieutenant kept the men at bay. Thankfully, it was well known, Max was close to Ilya as well. The last thing she wanted was to have to fight off men who thought it was their right to treat women as objects to be used and abused if it suited them.

Once she was gone, Max let out a short breath. The woman was impossible. But knowing that and even knowing Elena meant to goad her, Max couldn't help but wonder if what she said was true. Peter hadn't actually asked, but he did accept her offer to help him free his cousin. Would he have if he hadn't witnessed her skills during a fight? Maybe if she was all "oh my, I'm scared," he wouldn't have taken the time to even speak to her like an equal.

She suddenly became hot and, stepping into the tent, took off her backpack and coat. It didn't matter that she didn't fit in with these people; their fight wasn't hers, and she would be going back home soon anyway. There wasn't any reason to be there. She lifted the orb out of her backpack. It was in perfect working order. She could go back right then if she wanted to. But the trouble was, she wasn't sure she wanted to.

CHAPTER 9

Peter rounded the campfire and paused. Elena and Max were standing in the opening of their tent talking, and Max's expressions flitted across her face so openly; Peter could make out most of them easily. Confusion, annoyance, anger, but once Elena left, her chin dropped, and she rubbed her head as if whatever Elena said had gotten to her. Peter hoped Max was stronger than to listen to whatever spitefulness came out of Elena's mouth.

The woman was only there because her brother fought for the Whites and Kolya was Ilya's much-respected lieutenant. Both of whom agreed she added to the cause because she could go to places they couldn't, to scout around. They welcomed her in their midst, but Peter had already witnessed her true self in action. They had just rid a village of the Red menace when, instead of helping the villagers, Elena cut them with her poisonous tongue, demanding a young woman feed the soldiers. When the woman said she didn't have much, Elena grated, "Bring everything you have and be grateful you survived this day even if you don't survive another."

Peter had intervened and sent the woman back to her

house, telling her to stay there until the army had moved on. Elena had tried to laugh the episode off, saying the peasants should be more thankful for their freedoms.

He shook his head, wondering again what Elena had said to Max. He had the strongest notion she spoke of him and he didn't like it, but he could believe Elena would make it seem she and he were together, that they were romantically linked. He hoped the beautiful American hadn't believed anything the woman had to say.

"Ah, Peter, there you are."

Peter turned at Vanya's greeting. "You have been looking for me?"

"*Nyet*, not really. Just thought I'd like some company while I eat. Yegor is busy with some woman he met when we passed through the last village."

"Oh, so I am second choice then." Peter looked at Max's tent.

"*Nyet*, my friend, never." Vanya followed Peter's gaze. "Ah, the American has your thoughts, I see."

"She is different to any one I have ever met."

"But do you trust her? Elena is suggesting she may be a spy and has all but convinced her brother of it. Ilya listens to Kolya."

"I do trust her, Vanya. She is not a spy. I would stake my life on it."

Peter slid his gaze over the camp. The thought occurred to him then, while he believed with all his heart Max was not a spy for the Red Army, she could be an informant of sorts to the American government. She could fight, and her skills surpassed most of the Russian military, White or Red. Her training, wherever it occurred, had been top notch. And the main thing that concerned him was he knew she kept secrets. He just wished she trusted him enough to tell him. He may be able to help her in her quest.

"Good," Vanya said. "Because I like her. By the way, that is not what I came to speak to you about. Ilya is organizing a mission to free the royal family."

"The Romanovs?"

"Of course, the Romanovs. Where is your head tonight, Peter? Are you going to join such a mission?"

"I have already told Ilya, Karina's safety is my only concern."

Peter glanced once more in Max's direction and scratched his bearded chin.

Vanya let out a chuckle. "You like her a lot, don't you?"

"I admire her bravery, her fighting skills, that is all."

"So you have no romantic thoughts about the little warrior?"

"Of course not. We are at war and my mission is to free Karina. When I do, we will leave for Denmark. Maxine will either stay and fight or go back to America. There is no time for romance on the battlefield, my friend. No time at all."

"There is always time for romance." Vanya's gaze roamed down Max's body as she looked around the fire. "And if you have no attachment to the beauty, you won't mind my getting to know her better."

Peter didn't like the admiration in his eyes as he perused the girl. "There are plenty of pretty girls in the camp or in the villages and towns we pass through. Leave Maxine alone. She doesn't need you trying to seduce her at every turn."

Vanya raised an eyebrow then smiled. "May the best man win." And with that he hurried to Max's side, said something that made Max smile, and gave her his arm. Peter's throat closed as she slipped her arm around his and Vanya led her to the other side of the fire.

The only seat available was one next to Elena, so Peter had no choice but to sit there and eat his meal. One thing about the location he liked was that he could watch Max, watch how her expressive dark eyes either shone with mirth or clouded over something Vanya said. At first Peter thought Vanya told her something sad, but then the irritation flitting across her face told Peter his friend had started his seduction routine too early. He hid a smile as he wiped the stew from his mouth. Women usually went weak at the knees when Vanya showed them even some small attention. He was a handsome man, larger than Peter, but muscled, not fat.

"Peter," Elena whined beside him.

Without taking his eyes off Max, he said, "Huh?"

She laughed, too forcefully to Peter's mind, and hit him playfully on the arm. "You haven't listened to one word I've said."

"I apologize. What did you say?"

"Perhaps if you looked at me while we conversed, you would hear my words more clearly."

Peter turned to her just in time to see the hateful look she threw in Max's direction. "What is it you want, Elena?"

"I want you to pay me some attention instead of gawking at the spy."

"She isn't a spy and you know it. Stop spreading rumors."

"I don't know anything of the sort. She just appears in our midst. She is trained in the skills of fighting and we're supposed to believe she is lost from her guide? I don't think so. We need to be careful speaking of our plans around her. Ilya agrees."

Peter finished the last mouthful of bread and stood up. "Good night, Elena."

He caught Max's gaze as he strode toward her. "Would you like to take a stroll with me?"

"I'd love to." She put her plate down, took a drink and stood up. "Thank you for keeping me company, Vanya."

Vanya narrowed his eyes at Peter but didn't say anything.

Instead, he smiled at Max and bowed his head. "Good night, Maxine."

Peter gave Max his arm and once she'd wound her arm through his, he pulled her close into his side. "Did you enjoy your meal?"

"I was starving." She laughed. "They could have served mashed rat and I would have enjoyed it." She looked at his handsome profile, then watched where she stepped. "Where were you today?"

"Why? Did you miss me?"

"No, I just thought you were supposed to help with the horses."

"And I will, but today I met with Ilya. He has a plan for rescuing Karina and wanted to go through it with me."

"And?"

"And what?"

"And, is it a good plan?"

"Yes, very good."

"I'm glad."

As they strolled around the outskirts of the camp, Peter made small talk about the goings on back in Denmark, but the conversation petered out and they walked in comfortable silence. He enjoyed having her so close. The spicy perfume she wore when they first met was gone, but in its place her scent mixed with soap floated to his nostrils. He leaned sideways to get a better whiff.

Max stepped over a mound of melting snow. "So, what's the next move?"

"The next move?"

"Yeah, what is the army's next mission?"

Peter hesitated, but with her innocent eyes watching him he thought she was just making small talk, and as she was travelling with them, she would find out eventually anyway. "Ilya had word the Romanovs are imprisoned, not just under house arrest for their own safety. He has volunteered his regiment for the recovery of the Romanovs and depending on the timeline, I agreed to help." Peter smiled. "I hope you will still be with us then."

Max's hesitation, both in walk and in manner, confused Peter. She looked away, but not before he saw defeat in her eyes. He now wondered if she did know something they didn't. "Do you know something?"

"What? No. It's just a really hard mission when you will have your cousin with you by then. I thought you would take her to Denmark." She held Peter's arm tighter and smiled up at him. "So are we going to save your cousin soon?"

Peter knew she was changing the subject purposefully, but her open smile and interested gaze had him not really caring at that moment. "Ilya had word; they are moving Karina out of Kharkov in two days."

Max stopped and gazed at Peter. Her eyes were so full of worry, he wanted to hold her in his arms and tell her everything would be all right. But of course, she knew as well as him that rescuing Karina was dangerous for his cousin and for the saviors.

"Where to?" Max asked.

"We believe they are taking her to the Solovki prison camp on the Solovetsky islands. That is where her grandmother, the Grand Duchess Anericka, is being held."

"Where are the islands?"

"In the White Sea." Peter could tell by the way her eyes flickered from left to right she was thinking hard. It wouldn't take her long to realize this would probably be their only chance of saving Karina.

"The White Sea is a long way from here, and with Ilya set on being part of the mission to save the Romanovs from Tobolsk, you will have no way of going after her if you leave it

FROM CAFÉS TO COSSACKS

too long. We have to get her, Peter. This will be our only chance."

Peter's heart swelled in his chest at the concern for his cousin. This woman felt emotions deeply, and her understanding of how Peter needed to protect his cousin had to come from her own love for her family.

"You miss your family?" he asked.

"Yes, I do. They can be so irritating sometimes, but I love them and would risk my life to save them if they were in danger. So, yes, I know where you're coming from. Who is in charge of planning Karina's escape?"

As they strolled to the horse pen, Peter answered, "Ilya has developed an outstanding plan. If everyone does their bit, we will succeed."

Max stroked a fine bay's neck. The horse rumbled a neigh in appreciation. "Can I help?"

"I hoped you would." Peter had to concentrate to keep up with the conversation. Max's silhouette in the moonlight had captured his focus. Her wild dark hair pulled back in a single tie left her face open to the moonlight. He was struck by how much she looked like a pixie straight out of the Hans Christian Anderson story, *The Pixie and the Grocer*. Her facial features, blue eyes, high cheekbones, small but stubborn chin, were magical, and she too would save something as precious as art over money. Her expressions were wholly honest for the most part.

A voice at the back of Peter's mind whispered not to forget, she was keeping something from him. And he wouldn't, but at that moment the only thing he could think about was how he wanted to take her in his arms and kiss her pink lips.

She patted the horse's muzzle and he nibbled her open palm. She laughed. "I don't have anything for you." Wiping her hand down her thigh, she turned to Peter.

Even in the moonlight, he could see the color rising in her cheeks, but she didn't look away. He had all but ogled her and she should have slapped him; instead, she stood there, her cute nose flaring a little and the tip of her tongue darting out to wet her lips.

He stepped forward and could have sworn she did the same, then she was in his arms and his mouth crushed down on hers. Her arms folded around the back of his neck and she opened for him immediately and, like the shapely warrior she was, poked her tongue into his mouth, meeting his, ready to do battle.

She moaned, a soft, almost silent sound that had him answering with a low growl deep in his throat. He pulled her body into his so that every part of her melded into his form. Perfect.

She tasted faintly of the tomato she'd eaten earlier and of woman. Pure, delicious woman. As his hand left her back and began to roam to her waist, that whispering voice sounded in his brain. He hesitated. He couldn't take her there even if she was willing. If the stars granted such, he wanted their first time to be memorable. And he did want her for the first time, and the tenth and the hundredth. He doubted he could ever get enough of her, enough of those shapely curves melting into his hardened angles.

Reluctantly, he slowly broke the kiss and pulled his head back to look at her. Her eyes were shut, and her mouth open slightly. Her chin trembled, so too did her legs. He kept hold of her so she wouldn't fall. Her eyes opened, and he was once again drawn into those cavernous blue-black pools of lava. Passion had heated her eyes and she didn't even try to hide the desire within. Her gaze slid to his mouth and once again she wet her lips. Peter couldn't stop his body's reaction, and he bent down to take those lips once more.

"Peter," a voice called from far away. "Peter?"

Max pulled back with a gasp. Peter gave a shake of his head, pleading with his eyes for her not to go. But her gaze darted over his shoulder and all passion evaporated.

"There you are." Peter turned. Elena. "I've been looking for you everywhere."

"Why?"

CHAPTER 10

Max leaned on the makeshift fence—she didn't trust her shaky legs to hold her upright. Her brain, fogged and incoherent, let her body's reactions to Peter's kiss take over. She thrummed from head to toe and her lips tingled, feeling full and sensitive. Her logical brain heard Elena's voice, but her heart's rapid beat drowned out any other noise in her ears.

She had never reacted to someone kissing her like she had just reacted to Peter. Her body took over and all she wanted was to get closer to him, to taste him, to smell him. If she could, she would have crawled into his skin. Passion exploded when he touched her, her nerves all jangled and the woman in her screamed for him to get closer. Her response was immediate and, in her desire and need for him, she would have taken him then and there, not caring about the mud or horse droppings under her.

That thought startled her and she immediately eyed the muddy ground. Really, Max? You'd lie there? She shivered at the thought of it all.

She had to have time to think about her reactions, about

Peter, about everything. Elena's voice broke into her thoughts. "Ilya want to speak to you now."

"I'll be there in a moment," Peter said, taking Max's hand.

Max gave a shake of her head to clear some of the smoke from her brain and noted Elena's eyes narrow as they stared at her and Peter's hands entwined together.

Elena straightened her back and glowered at Peter. "He said, now."

"Go," he said. "I will be right behind you."

Peter turned to Max and brought her in for a hug. "I have to go. Please don't think badly of me."

Max snuggled into his warmth. "I couldn't."

"We'll talk later then."

Once Peter left, Max felt more alone than she ever had in her life. She walked on still shaky legs back to her tent. It was late, but with her body on high alert, she wasn't the least bit tired. He said they'd talk later, and she wasn't about to fall asleep until they did. Although Max wasn't really wanting to talk—she would much prefer to continue where they had left off. A rolling wave surged through her stomach at the thought of being in his arms once again and she smiled

Hours passed and still no Peter. No Elena either. Max stifled a yawn. Where was he? She thought she'd just lie down to wait, but she wouldn't close her eyes. Her head hit the pillow and that was the last thing she remembered.

※

BY THE TIME ILYA EXPLAINED HIS ORDERS, IT WAS TOO LATE to speak with Max, so Peter made his way to his tent and bed.

Before Peter slept, he relived the kiss, the kiss he'd had no intention of instigating, yet no way of controlling. He wanted to consume Max, and he wanted to never let her out of his arms. Blast the war. Why couldn't he have met her in peacetime, why couldn't he have met her in Denmark? He imagined them having picnics on the banks of the Gudena River and he smiled.

His thoughts that night were confusing and muddled—Max, Ilya, Max, the war, Max, home, Max, Karina, Max, and when he'd finally fallen asleep, his dreams were filled with the same things. Images of home, him and Max enjoying the summer riding horses along the Gudena River, Max and Karina, heads bent, giggling, Max dressed in the latest fashions summoning him into her bedroom.

His dreams had turned more romantic when, while he was stretched out on his back in his bed, Max jumped on him. covering him from neck to calf with her body, and kissed him.

Giving himself up to the experience, he was shocked awake when something—no, someone—hit his cheeks.

"About time you woke up," Vanya said.

Vanya stood over his cot fully dressed and ready to go into battle with his Berdan rifle a Finnish soldier had given him.

Peter tried to rub the sight of the big hairy Russian from his eyes. He wanted to return to his dream... to Max.

Peter closed his eyes and groaned, trying again to indulge in that latest dream. The weight of her body was still on him. He opened one eye. He felt his chest. Ah, thick. woolen, and heavy. His greatcoat. Vanya must have thrown it on him.

"It's time to break camp."

MAX SLEPT SOUNDLY UNTIL NOISES INTRUDED ON HER dreams. Her first thought was Peter and her eyes snapped open. The noises were voices and they were right outside the tent.

She sat up and listened but couldn't place Peter's voice

among the speakers, some talking quickly in Russian and others shouting orders, also in Russian.

Horses' hooves trotted past and heavy armored vehicles rattled in the distance. Max rubbed her eyes. Still in her clothes from the night before, she got up and tried to stretch the kinks out of her body as she opened the tent flap.

The morning sun was trying to peer over the mountains, but the clouds blocked its light.

The whole camp was on the move and Ilya was making his way toward her.

"Ah, Maxine," Ilya said as he stopped in front of her. "We are moving out."

"Now?"

"*Da,* and you must go home." He tilted his head to the inside of the tent. "Take your orb and go."

Men started removing the tent pegs from Max's tent. "Wait," she said, putting her hands up to stop them. "At least let me get my stuff first."

"Come back for this one," Ilya said to the soldier.

She made a face that said she didn't want to go but said, "Well, I guess this is it then."

They both stood scanning the disappearing campsite in silence for a moment, and Max spotted Peter walking along the row of cars to the side of the camp.

She and Ilya turned to face one another, and both went to speak at the same time.

They laughed and Ilya said, "I wish I had more time to spend with you. Please ask Briana to send you back in a time of peace." He smiled and Max thought she caught a glimmer of pink blush his cheeks for a second. "I cannot leave without telling you a confession."

Max tipped her head to the side. "A confession?"

"*Da*, I thought perhaps you had come to find a husband, a love, like your sisters. I thought that was why Briana had sent you to me, but then I saw you weren't interested in me that way. Then I thought perhaps it was Andrei you were sent here for, but again, you weren't any friendlier with him than you were with me."

"What? No. I'm not here to find a husband. Don't get me wrong, I'm glad for my sisters, but that's not what I needed—I needed to find what I want to do with the rest of my life. That's why I hoped I could stay here longer, to see what my purpose was."

"Are you sure it is not Peteor who has taken your heart?"

"No way." *At least I don't think so.* "But I did like looking after the horses and I think that's what I will do. Study veterinary science and specialize in the treatment of horses."

"You didn't need to travel back into the past to discover your love for horses."

"No, but I would have just probably owned them like I do now. If you hadn't given me the chance to spend time with the Kabardas, I wouldn't know what it felt like to save a horse and to enjoy seeing that they were all healthy."

She gave him a hug. With his greatcoat on, he was even rounder than usual, and her arms didn't reach around his back, so she held on to the coat at his sides and rested her head on his chest. "Thank you for that."

He wrapped his arms around her and gave her a gentle squeeze. "I am glad you found your way and I hope to see you again."

"Me too." She moved back and glanced inside the tent.

"*Da*, it is best if you disappear out of sight of the soldiers."

Max giggled. "I think you're right there."

He kissed her on both cheeks. "Goodbye, Maxine."

She gave him another hug. "Goodbye, my friend."

Stepping inside, she turned. Ilya was already walking away with his head bent.

She looked out over the horse enclosure. Everything was

gone, the fence, the feed sacks, the horses. She made a small sucking noise. She would miss riding Girl—she was a sturdy, big-hearted horse.

She backed up into the tent. She hadn't noticed before that Elena wasn't there, nor had her cot been slept in. Max bit her lip. Had someone forgotten to tell her something? The last time she saw Elena was after Peter's kiss. She smiled at the memory. But then he left with Elena to see Ilya.

A cough sounded behind her. She spun around. A tall soldier stood to attention. "Miss, we are breaking camp. This tent is coming down."

Max looked around the tent and spied her backpack. "Hang on." She quickly filled it with the few clothes Peter had rummaged up for her and nodding to the soldier, she left the tent. Ilya wouldn't mind if she said goodbye to her new friends.

Slinging the pack over her shoulder, she scanned the disappearing camp in search for someone she recognized. Peter was nowhere in sight. Nor was Elena, but Vanya and Yegor were chatting next to a fire.

Making her way to them, she guessed something happened during the night to change Ilya's mind about when they were to continue their march. Intel that she'd like to know about.

"Good morning," Max said as she joined them.

"We wondered if you were going to be folded into the tent still asleep," Yegor said.

His cheeky grin told Max he was playing with her.

She picked up a tin cup and poured hot coffee into it from the coffee pot. The heat through her gloves was comforting. "What's going on?"

Vanya refilled his cup. "The regiment has orders to—"

"Leave," Yegor cut in, giving Vanya a strange look.

Max sipped her coffee, trying to read Yegor's silent communication with his friend. She had a feeling he was admonishing Vanya for being about to tell her where the army was going. She sucked on her bottom lip. It seemed they no longer trusted her.

Peter joined them and took the cup Vanya offered him. "We will only have time for a quick breakfast, then we'll be on our way."

"To Kharkov?" Max asked.

He nodded, his heated gaze melting Max's ire.

He turned to the two men. "Vanya, you and Yegor get the car ready."

Max watched the soldiers head toward a small armored vehicle. "Is the whole army going with you?"

A wave of irritation swept over Peter's face. "No. Including me? We have three."

"But I thought Ilya was leading this operation?"

"He was, but General Krasnov has countermanded his orders and sent him on an urgent mission."

"Where to?"

"I am sorry, Max, but that is classified."

"Oh, okay." Max turned her head so he wouldn't see the hurt in her eyes. That he didn't trust her either cut through her heart so painfully she had to stop herself from holding on to her chest. She blinked back the silly tears his words brought on. Wait. He said three of them were rescuing Karina. If Vanya and Yegor were the other two, Max wondered what happened to Elena. Pasting on her all-business face, she turned back to Peter. "Where is Elena?"

"She has volunteered to go with Ilya."

"I thought she wanted to help you free Karina?"

Peter's eyes flickered to the quickly disappearing tables. "I did too." He let out a laugh. "Quickly, or there will be no food left."

Once they'd eaten, Max looked about for Ilya. She had a

bad feeling in her stomach; she had to know where he was going. "Where is Ilya now?"

"I don't know, but aren't you going with him?"

"That would be a no."

"You are still coming with us?"

Max bit her bottom lip. He only had two other soldiers to go with him to save his cousin. Maybe she could help Peter free Karina somehow. Peter had said he would like her to go with him, but then Ilya said to go home. She glanced at Peter and quickly looked down at her boots. If something happened, she could always use the orb just like Ilya told her to, couldn't she? He didn't say exactly when she had to go, not really, he just said she had to. She knew she was being pedantic, but hey, it suited her at that moment.

"Is something wrong?" Peter asked.

Max gazed into his concerned eyes and smiled widely. "No, nothing, I'm ready whenever you are."

"Good."

Before anything though, she had to find out where Ilya and his army were going. "So where do you think Ilya is right now? I'd like to say goodbye."

"He will be in one of the lead vehicles."

Max shot up and ran to the head of the line of foot and horse soldiers, tanks and armored cars.

"Ilya," she called as she passed every car.

He ducked his head out of the third car in line. "Maxine." He hopped out and stood waiting for her.

"What are you doing here? I thought you had returned home. It's no longer safe for you here."

"I know. I'm worried about you. Where are you going?"

"General Krasnov has ordered my troop to Tobolsk. The Romanovs are there."

"Oh, Ilya." Max couldn't help the tears filling her eyes.

How could she let him go without telling him how useless his mission was?

Ilya hugged her and whispered in her ear. "*Nyet*. Do not say anything. The outcome of the war is already written in the pages of your history, but believe me when I say, I have no intention of dying." He stepped back and held her hands, shaking them and smiling. "I will see my family once more, and Mark told me the last time we met; we will meet again in the summer of 1920."

"He did?" Relief had Max smiling stupidly.

Ilya nodded. "*Da*, and I hope to see you again, my lovely Maxine."

"I hope so too, Ilya. Please tell Mom and Dad how much I love them when you see them?"

"*Da*. Now go home and think of this war no more."

Max gave him a hug and kissed his cheek. "Goodbye, my friend."

Ilya's driver drove off as soon as Ilya climbed back in the car. The main company began heading out, horsemen, armored vehicles, tanks, and foot soldiers.

Max walked back to what was left of the breakfast area, and she couldn't help smiling. Ilya would be safe. Now all she had to do was help Peter's cousin, and then she could go home happy. Maybe Bree could find a way to reset the orb so she could come back in the summer of 1920 to meet with Ilya and her parents.

CHAPTER 11

Peter opened a map and showed Max where they were going to go. "We will skirt the edges of the city and once near the small hamlet on the other side, where our intelligence says Karina is being held, we will go on foot."

That made sense to Max. No point in shouting out their arrival. "How many are guarding her?"

"Our intel reports five at any given time. There are more but they take shifts. Three outside and two inside. Apparently, they don't see Karina as important. It should be an easy mission."

Max glanced at Peter's profile. His strong square jaw tightened, hinting he didn't really believe that. Neither did Max. "So what aren't you telling me?"

"I can't fault the report, it comes from trusted intel, but something about the easiness of the situation doesn't sit well with me. I have seen nothing in this war to make me think the Bolsheviks care less about one royal than another. They hate all, and I fear they would do anything to rid Russia of every last one of us."

"That's most likely true."

The city was large, but the apartment Ilya had arranged for them was next door to where Karina was being held prisoner. Peter pointed to what was labeled "Shopping District." "We won't go hungry while we are there."

Max was relieved to hear that. She hadn't noticed anyone packing any provisions for the mission and wondered about food.

Peter and Max walked to the one remaining car and Max ogled the vehicle that was no longer really a car but a tank. The domed top slid back and Yegor's head and shoulders popped out of the narrow opening. He took command of a machine gun turret that looked like it could rotate three hundred and sixty degrees.

Peter chuckled beside her and she looked at him. He held out his hand toward the car. "This is our very own Austro-Daimler Panzerwagen."

Vanya was already in the driver's seat. Peter went in first and when Max joined him, there wasn't anywhere for her to sit. "You'll have to sit here," Peter said, patting his leg. "The tank was only built to carry three, driver, commander and gunner."

Max raised her eyebrows. He could have warned her. His brown eyes darkened but filled with humor as he patted his leg again. She bit her bottom lip. He was enjoying her discomfort. She shrugged. *What has to be, has to be,* she told herself. She twisted and perched on one of his legs sideways so her legs had room between the seat and the door. Vanya pulled the driver's metal door shut with a bang and drove, lurched really, out of the camp.

Max held on to the back of the driver's seat to keep her balance. Peter put his arms around Max's waist and pulled her over so her bottom had the comfort of both his legs.

"There, that's better," he said. Keeping one arm around

her middle, he gently pushed her head against his shoulder. "It's a long drive."

Max sighed. She liked being close to him, smelling his pine tree scent. She hadn't gotten much sleep the night before because she was trying to wait up, and she must have dozed off on Peter's shoulder.

She woke with a start as Vanya stopped the car abruptly and Peter's arms tightened around her. "We're here," Vanya said.

"Where?" Max said sleepily.

"Kharkov," Peter said.

Once out of the vehicle, Max looked to Peter for the direction. The shoulder of his uniform was damp. Ugh. Subconsciously, she wiped her mouth. She must have dribbled in her sleep. He gave her a quick side hug, then took the lead with Vanya. Yegor waved his boney hand at her, indicating she should go next.

Max took in the street. People were coming and going in and out of shops. Some of the buildings shared side walls, while others had a narrow lane separating them. The shops filled the buildings' bottom floors and if they weren't there to rescue someone, Max would have loved to visit some of the quaint stores, especially the bakery they passed before Peter disappeared around the side of a building. Max breathed in the yeasty scent of fresh bread as she hurried to keep up with Peter and Vanya.

Max and Yegor followed a narrow lane that opened out on another street. They all stopped at a crossroad until Peter signaled for them to go. They hurried across the road and into another through lane.

Mid-morning bustle in the streets covered their progress. Max kept a look out for any Red Army soldiers, but as they went from street to street, and away from the shopping district into a residential area, she saw none.

Ilya had given them an apartment to stay until they were ready to act. Once they climbed the dark stairwell to the third floor, Max relaxed and walked to the only window in the room. It overlooked the small house where Karina was kept.

Even from her vantage point, the only soldiers she spied were the four on guard duty. One marched back and forth in the front of the house and two on either side did the same backwards and forwards rounds while, Max presumed, the fourth soldier guarded the back of the house. In another time, the house would have been pretty, with flowered gardens around its perimeter, but the gardens had all gone to weeds now, brown, and ugly, telling a sorrowful story of neglect.

THE NEXT DAY, YEGOR AND VANYA LEFT TO SCOUT THE area around the apartment block.

Peter was looking out the window while Max couldn't find any coffee but she did find the packet of black tea leaves. *Why couldn't they have tea bags?* But she had watched Vanya make tea the night before so found the teapot. Once the kettle of water had boiled, she poured the hot liquid over the tea leaves in the pot and immediately poured Peter a cup. She handed him the cup.

"Thanks," he said. Sipping the hot tea, he looked at her with wide eyes as he swallowed. "How much tea did you use?"

"Three spoonful's, the same as Vanya did last night."

"Did you let it brew?"

Max frowned. "Huh?"

"Did you let it stand for a couple of moments, so the tea seeped into the water."

"Ah, that would be a no." She took the cup from him. "It's been standing awhile now, I'll get you another one."

Giving him another cup of tea, Max asked, "When do we go in?"

"An hour or so after dark." He sipped his tea. "Ah, that's better. The shift changes should occur at midnight and by the look of boredom on their faces, these ones are ready to be done with their duties. Hopefully, they won't be fully alert."

Max drank from her cup all the while wishing it were coffee and gazed out of the window. One of the side soldiers tripped on an exposed tree root. A root that had obviously been there all day, and one he should have been aware of. "Yeah, they're tired all right."

Peter put his cup down and came up behind her, wrapping his arms around her waist. Max leaned back without conscious thought. He kissed her neck and she tilted her head to give him better access to that spot where her neck met her shoulder. He accepted the invitation and shivers rolled down her back in waves. At the same time, her legs near buckled under her.

He turned her around, but the change in movement had Max gaining some semblance of intelligence. She wriggled out of his arms and backed up. "The boys could come in any moment."

Peter stepped forward. She backed up a step, but the wall stopped any further movement away. His eyes darkened as he gazed at her lips. Before she could do anything, he scooped her up in his arms and kissed her. Without thought she flung her arms around his neck and melted into him.

Somewhere in her brain, she knew they shouldn't take their passion any further. She didn't have birth control and in her state of ardor, she wouldn't insist he look after that little detail.

He broke off the kiss and began nibbling his way down her neck to that spot where Max lost her head. There was no hope for them. She had to stop this. He looked at her, piercing her with his need. How could she deny him, deny herself? They might never get another chance, and at least it would be something she could remember for the rest of her days.

Peter scooped her up and carried her to the bedroom, kissing her at the same time. Just as he was about to step over the threshold, the outer door opened.

"Has something happened?" Vanya asked.

Peter dropped Max onto her feet, but as if understanding her imbalance, he held on to her waist so she wouldn't fall. Max heard the almost silent groan in his throat as he rubbed his face. "Why?"

Vanya looked from one to the other. "I thought... Maxine." He chuckled. "*Nyet.* Never mind. My mistake."

Max was sure she had turned bright red from the heat in her face. She turned away and hurried to the bedroom window, making out as if that was where she was going all along.

She gazed unseeing at the street below and shook her head. She had to stop falling into Peter's arms every time they were alone. If Vanya hadn't walked in when he did, she would have made a terrible mistake. She couldn't let her base desires take over; she had to keep her head straight or she wouldn't be any use to the rescue effort.

She touched her lips and a shiver ran down her back. Peter was a great kisser and although it was obvious, he wanted her, there was no way Max could let that happen. Sure she was attracted to him, but did she love him? And even if she did, what difference would that have made? She promised Garrett she would return, and there was no way she wanted to live in the Russia of the past. No. It just wouldn't work, and she wasn't going to give herself to someone she'd never see again. One day perhaps she'd find a man to love, and she didn't want her time in Russia to ruin that chance.

She decided to head to the bathroom, clean up and return her mind and body to the mission at hand.

※

THEY WATCHED THE HOUSE ALL DAY AND MAX NOTED THE boredom in the guards. They did their duty, but had become lax, stopping and chatting together whenever they met at the corners. They didn't seem to be alert or even on the lookout for any trouble. Max peered out the window in the fading light. Perhaps they thought they were untouchable?

Yegor brought some bread and sausage in as the sun set. When they'd finished eating, Peter led them out of the apartment and down the stairs. Once outside, they snuck into the narrow lane that separated the apartment block from a row of shops. Peter signaled with his finger for Yegor and Vanya to go. They would go down the street and once they were far enough along, they would cross the road and circle around behind the neighboring houses. He and Max would go in the opposite direction, Peter splitting off first, and Max was to follow to guard his rear.

"Are you ready?" Peter asked Max before she could take her position.

She nodded. He leaned in and kissed her cheek. "Be careful."

"Always." Max followed Peter, keeping as close as she could to the apartment building. She paused in a darkened alcove made by a small balcony above while Peter crept past her to the next street corner.

Yegor's call, a soft bird's song, floated down the quiet street. Peter hurried across the road and disappeared down alongside the fence. Once he was out of sight, Max followed.

Another bird's song sounded, and she scampered over the fence. Her target, perfectly situated, was walking away with his back to her. She covered the distance between them in seconds and hit the guard on the base of his skull with her knuckles, hard. He fell instantly. She quickly took his rifle and pulled the cloth and ties from her pockets. Tying his hands and ankles together, she then forced one of the cloths into his mouth and tied the other one around his head, over his large mouth.

Keeping down, she crept to the back of the house. Peter had taken his guard down and left him in a similar pose to hers. A glint of his even white teeth showed under the window's light, telling Max he was smiling at her. He crooked his index finger to indicate she should join him. She did and, having faith that Yegor and Vanya were doing the same at the front of the house, Max followed Peter through the unlocked back door.

Two soldiers, sitting at the small square table in the center of the kitchen, gaped at them. One gained his senses first and leapt up to get his rifle leaning against the kitchen sink. Peter was on him before he could reach it, but the soldier was quick and knocked Peter to the ground. Max aimed her gun at the other soldier, who instantly raised his hands. She chewed the side of her mouth. Something about this was too easy.

Peter landed a punch on his opponent's jaw, knocking him out.

Still aiming the rifle at the seated soldier, Max sidled around to the door opening into a short hallway. Scuffles could be heard in the next room, and Max guessed Yegor and Vanya were there.

"Where is Karina?" Peter asked, pointing his rifle at the seated soldier. The soldier looked at him in confusion. Peter spoke again in Russian, and Max guessed he repeated his question because the soldier pointed to the ceiling.

Peter went about tying the soldiers; the unconscious one he left on the floor and the other he tied to the chair.

Someone's boot clicked in the hall. Max snapped her gun around and almost depressed her finger on the trigger before she realized it was Yegor. "I could have killed you," she said, hesitating before moving her gun back toward the conscious soldier. Yegor also kept his pistol up, ready to use if needed. "Why didn't you alert us to your presence?" Max said.

She knew what he would say before he said it. She knew she was being difficult.

"How was I to know you had prevailed in here? I could have been walking into the enemy's camp for all I knew."

Max re-aimed her gun at the soldier. He was right. The poor man couldn't see through walls.

"All clear," he said to Peter, but not before shooting Max a contemptuous look.

"Watch them," Peter said to Max as he left the room.

"Wait," Max called out after him.

He turned and raised his brows.

"Don't you think this is way too easy?"

"What do you mean?"

"I mean," she waved the gun around the room, "this, all this. What? Do you think Karina is waiting in her prison room all alone and you will just go in and take her?"

Vanya pushed two bound soldiers before him into the kitchen, forcing Peter to step aside. "She's right, Peter. Something doesn't feel right."

Max shot him a thank-you look.

"All right. Tie them to the chairs."

All the soldiers were slim, except the kitchen guard Max had overpowered. He was short and round with blond hair. The skinniest one had a short beard.

Once Yegor appeared happy with their binds, Peter said, "You and Vanya come with me, guns ready. Max, don't take your eyes off them."

"I won't."

Once they were alone, the kitchen soldier's gaze roved over Max. The man was curious but not scared. Peter hadn't gagged him, and he said something in Russian. Max tried to pretend she was just ignoring him, not that she couldn't understand him. He spoke again, and this time urgency laced his voice.

The soldiers Vanya had captured were gagged, but one of them shook his head enough to lower the material. He said something to his comrade. They talked quickly to one another.

Max continued to ignore them, wondering if she could kill them if she had to. She was sure the kitchen guard knew she was out of place there and that he'd already told his fellow guards. As soon as his other comrades found him, he would tell them all about the strange woman who helped rescue the Lady Karina.

Not ten minutes later, Peter appeared with a young woman followed by a laughing Yegor. Karina, Max guessed, had the same straight regal nose as Peter and her eyes were as brown as her hair. Her loose-fitting orange dress fell to her ankles from a wide band under her breasts. Max looked her up and down. Not the best outfit for escaping a prison, but at least the long sleeves would keep her mildly warm.

Vanya chuckled as he pushed a soldier so young, he appeared hardly out of school into the kitchen. The man's lip was bleeding and swollen.

"What's so funny?" Max asked.

"That's enough, Yegor," Peter said, turning his gaze to Max. "I'll fill you in later, but now, we have to go."

Karina spoke in Russian to the young soldier, who replied with a slight smile. Max soon caught up. It was clear he and Karina had bonded.

After retying the binds on all the soldiers and making sure their gags stayed in place, Peter led them out of the house via the back door. They climbed fence after fence until they were at the crossroads.

The plan was for Max to stay back, guarding the rear while Yegor and Vanya lurked to either side, and that's the way they made their way down the street, keeping to the shadows as much as possible. It was too dangerous to go back to the apartment, so they had to make their way to the armored car, and they had to hurry before the change of guards.

Max used all her covert skills to stay hidden as she followed Peter and Karina. Yegor and Vanya must have had the same talent because she couldn't see or hear them. She hoped they were still there.

Shadows in Max's peripheral vision had her snapping her head to the side. She burrowed closer to the wall. Black silhouettes exploded from the apartment building on the corner. Max smashed her lips together to stop a surprised gasp escaping. There was about eight of them and they ran after Peter.

Max's heart leapt in her throat. *Peter.* She hoisted her gun and, using both hands to hold the weight, she scampered after them.

She opened her mouth to let out the warning call but before she could make a sound, blackness enveloped her and her mind spun. No, not her mind, her entire body was spinning. Blast, she was falling through space and time. Her stomach convulsed and anger surged through her veins, heating them to boiling temperature.

CHAPTER 12

Max stopped spinning and although she landed on her feet, she bent and held her knees, and screamed.

Garrett rushed to her. "Where are you hurt?"

She pushed him away. "I'm not hurt. Send me back." Her eyes hardened and her pupils dilated in anger and fear. "Send me back now."

Garrett gaped at her, confusion in every change of expression. "But we agreed, two days, Max, and it's been two days."

She jumped to her feet. "I don't care. Send me back."

Bree hurried down the stairs. "What's happening?"

Max rounded on her. "You have to send me back to the exact spot I left, and you have to do it now."

Garrett moved toward her but stopped short as Max took up her fighting stance. She balanced on parted feet with one more forward than the other. One arm straight out in front of her and the other waiting close to her chest, her fingers waving in the air as if they had a mind of their own and they wanted to touch something, hurt something. She didn't like scaring her little brother, but Garrett had to know how angry she was if he was going to let Bree send her back.

"What. Am. I. Doing. Here?"

Garrett held his hands up in surrender. "I made Bree bring you home. It was dangerous there."

Bree coughed. "Your brother was worried about you, Maxine. Are you saying you weren't in danger?"

"Oh, I was in danger all right. So was everyone in my team and if I don't go back, they'll all be killed."

"Max," Garrett said, his voice calm and reasonable sounding. "It's 2025. Those people, your team, are in 1917. They have been dead a long time."

Max took in a sharp intake of breath. They were dead. She slowly lowered her arms and relaxed her stance. Getting her head around the fact that Garrett was right, that there and now, all of them were probably already dead, either from fighting an already lost war or from old age. If anyone she'd met there was alive, they'd be well over one hundred years old. Not knowing their exact ages in 1917, she couldn't say how old exactly, but she realized it was impossible even with today's medicines for anyone to survive that long. And why was she even trying to work it out anyway? She was still twenty-six. She closed her eyes and tried to get her brain functioning again, but Peter's image firmly embedded itself in her mind.

Even knowing from where she stood now, what was done was done, she still wanted to save Peter.

Garrett came forward quickly and pulled her into a hug. "It's all right. You're home now."

Max let herself enjoy his comfort for a few seconds before she pushed him away. "Thanks for protecting me, little brother, but I can take care of myself." She peered at him. "I still want to go back."

"It doesn't have to be this exact second, Max." Bree moved to the stairs. "How about I go and make some coffee."

As soon as she said coffee, Max could almost smell it, and her mouth watered at the thought of real espresso instead of that diesel-smelling stuff the Russians called coffee.

Bree was right, she could send her back to the very moment she ripped her from at any time. But even knowing that, her heart still raced, and the thought of Peter being injured or killed had her in a cold sweat.

Max inhaled and exhaled three slow deep breaths. She would save Peter, she had to, but she had to calm down. She needed to convince Garrett she needed to go back. The last thing she wanted was for them to part on bad terms, especially if she never saw him again.

As soon as the basement door shut, Garret said, "I don't think Bree is telling us the whole truth. She's hiding something, I'm positive of it."

Max turned back to Garrett. "I want to go back."

"Are you mad? There's a war going on."

"I know." Max smiled and went on to tell Garrett everything that had happened to her since she'd landed in 1917.

After she'd finished, he said, "You know the Whites lose, don't you?"

"I know, but they weren't all killed. A lot of the people from the Triple Entente," at Garrett's confused expression, she explained, "that's what they called the agreement between the allied forces of Russia, Great Britain, the United States, well, lots of countries anyway."

"America?"

"Yeah, we were mainly there to re-establish the Eastern Front. But enough of the history lesson. Peter isn't even supposed to be a part of the war, he's there to rescue his cousin and take her back to Denmark." Max patted his hand. "You know I can't close my eyes to what I believe is the right thing to do and if I can help Peter and his cousin at least get to England, then I have to try. I hate that she was caught up in all of this. She's not much more than a kid and she had no say who her parents were."

Garrett threw his hands in the air in defeat. "Fine, but what about Bree and her secrets?"

She gave a shake of her head. "I don't think she's doing anything wrong. She loves us as much as we love her, and she's much too nice to do anything that might hurt any of us. Maybe there's something her mother and our mother arranged that we don't know about." Max paused for a moment to get her thoughts straight. Ilya came to her mind and she was thankful Garrett kept silent and waited for her to go on. "Now that I said that, Ilya, he was my contact, said a couple of things that make me think our parents knew exactly what they were doing when they asked us to all go back in time. Bree must know something because I asked to go back to Peter the Great's time and she sent me right into the middle of the revolution, but she also gave me the right contact name for 1917, not 1699, and I'm sure the contacts would have been different people or Ilya is a lot older than he looks."

She laughed but stopped suddenly, scared that she would melt down into hysterical laughter. She had to get herself under control. In her mind she pictured Peter and the group frozen in time, waiting for her return. That made her feel better. They would stay that way until she went back.

Bree's footfalls sounded coming down the stairs.

Max grinned. "But I don't care about any of that now, I want a quick coffee and then I'm gone."

CHAPTER 13

Peter kept Karina close. He was ecstatic he had gotten her out safely but was still worried that it was too easy. Fearing a trap, he took a different route than what was planned. Hurrying his cousin around the corner and into a lane that headed in the direction of the vehicle, he heard a shot ring out behind him. He stopped abruptly. Max. But had she fired or was she fired upon?

"Quickly," he said to Karina, pointing down the lane. "Run down there and hide behind those dumpsters."

She took off and Peter edged to the entrance of the laneway. Black-clothed soldiers sprang out of the corner apartment building, firing at Vanya and Yegor. Firing their pistols behind them, they zigzagged with their heads down, running toward the same lane he had chosen.

Peter emptied his rifle at the advancing soldiers. Some fell but he missed most of his targets.

Vanya and Yegor stopped beside him. "Both of you, get Karina out of here," Peter said.

"Vanya can go, I'm staying," Yegor said.

"No, you can drive the car as well as me. I'll stay," Vanya argued.

Shots zipped down the lane.

"There's no time to argue," Peter growled. "Yegor go, before she is found."

Vanya knelt below Peter's rifle and pulled his Berdan from his back and fired.

Reloading, Peter fought to keep his mind on the attack. All he could think of was Max. Pictures of her lying dead or dying between him and the soldiers filled his mind.

A shot whizzed past Peter's shoulder. He folded into the wall, firing his rifle without seeing any targets. More shots exploded throughout the night. His body wilted. It sounded like the entire Red Army had converged on this spot. Peter's rifle listed. He and Vanya couldn't take out a whole battalion.

Vanya let out a war cry and kept firing. One leg bobbed on the ball of its foot as if in excitement. Peter thought his friend meant to go out in a blaze of glory. The least he could do was the same. He readjusted his grip on the trigger and held the stack into his shoulder and fired. Praying Max was safe and hiding somewhere, he couldn't focus through the moisture filling his eyes.

Vanya started laughing.

Peter glanced at him. Was he mad? Had it all finally pushed him over the edge of sanity?

Vanya stopped firing, stood up, and slapped Peter on the shoulder. "We got them."

Peter shook his head and followed his friend's charged gaze. More dark-clothed soldiers swarmed over the bodies of the dead or dying. White armbands told Peter they weren't the enemy as he had feared—they were White Army soldiers. They quickly collected all the enemies' weapons as one of the soldiers strode toward him and Vanya.

"Are you well?" he spoke in Russian.

"*Da*," Peter said, also speaking in Russian. "How did you know?"

The young man pushed his blond hair out of his face and grinned. "We have our sources, Comrade. You can fulfill your mission now; we'll look after this."

Peter looked at the scene. Trucks were already being loaded with the enemy. The street would be empty within minutes. He clasped the man's hand. "Thank you, but I would like to know how you knew about the trap."

And it was a trap, of that Peter was certain.

"Informants," was all the man said. He shook Peter's hand. "Go before the whole city wakes up."

As the soldier spoke, he gazed up at a window and nodded. Peter followed his gaze. Someone quickly closed the curtains.

Understanding the urgency, Peter spoke quickly, "Have you seen a woman dressed in Whites' clothing?" He raised his arm and held out his hand at shoulder height. "She's about this high, dark hair and big blue eyes."

The soldier's eyes flitted in all directions. "No."

"Please look for her."

"I will, now go." He pointed to an armored car. "Follow them. Ilya is waiting for our return."

Peter nodded to Vanya and they hurried down the lane and rushed into the waiting vehicle, Vanya taking his place at the gun and Karina sitting on the only other seat. Before Peter could settle himself on the floor, Yegor accelerated away from the city.

❧

They soon arrived at the campsite, near a small hamlet only about ten miles from the city. Ilya and Elena sat at a fire warming themselves with only a small regiment circling and guarding the perimeter.

Elena offered Peter a hot mug. The coffee was only just warm, but Peter gulped the liquid down.

"How did you know?" Peter asked Ilya as he sat down on the log opposite the man.

"My scouts sent back word that your mission was compromised, and the enemy planned a trap. I went back to warn you, but you'd already left. Kolya volunteered to lead the army into Kharkov."

Elena had a glint in her eye, a look that concerned Peter. One he had seen before when she won a card game of Scat. She was pleased about something.

"Where is Maxine?" Elena asked.

Peter clamped his lips together. And there it was. She was glad Max wasn't with them. "We lost her in the battle. Ilya's man is looking for her."

At that, Ilya stood up. "She was with you?"

"Yes." Peter said the word slowly, wondering why Ilya appeared anxious.

Ilya's gaze flitted around the camp before resting on Peter. "I believe Maxine is safe. We will stay here until my army returns. You are welcome to join us at the inn." He looked at Karina. "My lady? Would you like to come with me?"

Karina leant into Peter's side. *"Nyet."*

Ilya smiled kindly at her. "I understand." He bowed and left.

Peter sat at a table in the inn with Karina sleeping on the bench beside him, waiting for Ilya's army to return from Kharkov. Ilya and his men were drinking and flirting with the serving women. They acted happy, but a solemnity lingered beneath the surface. He glanced at his cousin. Poor thing was exhausted and frightened, but she was safe, and he would do everything in his power to get her to Denmark. She was much younger than Peter, and he had wondered if she would even remember him. Thankfully, she had, and she seemed to trust him. He stood up and walked to the window, looking for any sign of the army's return.

Elena flitted from table to table, talking, laughing and flirting. Every now and then, she would seek Peter out. She would have known he was watching her. And he was watching her, but not because he was interested in her, because he wanted to know where she was if, no, *when* Max came back. Peter took confidence in Ilya's assurance that she was safe.

But he didn't want Elena accusing the lovely American of any wrongdoing without him present to defend her. Every now and then she would start humming.

As he sat back, Peter retraced everything that had happened before Max disappeared. They were moving down the street, Max in the rear. She crossed the street and hid in an alcove watching them get Karina away. He saw Max move to the next alcove, but that was the last time he saw her. She was there one moment and gone the next. The thought that the Bolsheviks had captured her cramped his chest. He would rather she left of her own free will then to be taken prisoner by the Reds. They weren't known for dealing gently with their prisoners.

"That woman has gone," Elena said, sliding into the seat beside Peter. "She ran away from the fight. She is a coward and not woman enough for you." Elena stroked Peter's arm. "We are good together, *da?*"

Peter took her hand off his arm and moved back. "We are not together, Elena. I am taking Karina back to Denmark and we will never see one another again."

She blanched, hurt springing in her eyes. Peter felt bad about hurting her until her gaze changed to a glare of hateful anger. "Maxine has gone. Forget about her, Peter. I am here and I am willing to keep you warm. She taunts you until you slaver over her like she's a dog in heat. She's..."

The sound of engines drowned out her last words and Peter hurried out of the inn. Watching, searching as the men piled out of the vehicles.

He waited until everyone had disembarked and made their way to the camp, everyone except the leader, Kolya, who, with his man, was the last to leave their vehicle. Kolya handed a board to the soldier and, leaving the soldier there, made his way past Peter.

"Wait, Kolya." Peter grasped onto his arm to stop him going any further. Kolya stopped and glared at Peter's hand. Peter let go. "Did you find a small woman, black hair, standing this high?" He held his hand at chest height to signify her height.

"*Da*. We cleaned up the mess. Found the woman. She is prisoner in there." He pointed to the vehicle he had just emerged from.

"What?" Peter ran to the car and peered inside. He found Max's eyes staring back at him. She smiled and held her hands out at shoulder height, shrugging. He understood she didn't know why she was being held and he chuckled, so happy was he that she was safe and within his reach. But he had to get her out of there, to make sure it was indeed her and not someone who looked like her.

"Wait there," he shouted at her. Then turned and marched into the inn, straight to Ilya. Kolya sat at the same table drinking wine.

"Ilya," Peter said, glaring at Kolya. "Maxine is being held as a prisoner."

"Is that true?" Ilya asked Kolya.

"*Da*. She was armed and ready to fire on me and my men."

"Nonsense," Peter said. "She wouldn't have if she knew you were with us."

"We had our armbands on." Kolya held his cup up for more wine.

Elena was there within seconds with another mug. "So, you caught her?" she asked Kolya with a frown.

"She is not the enemy," Peter said, his temper rising with the tempo of his pulse in his temples. "Ilya, please tell him to release her."

Ilya stood up. "I will talk with her."

Peter paced the front of the inn for what seemed like hours but when he checked his watch, it had only been twenty-five minutes. Not for the first time, Peter wondered about Max and Ilya's relationship. As far as he knew they had never met before, but their constant conversations back at the earlier camp, and the silent exchanges Peter had noticed, had him thinking they indeed did know one another—well.

He then worried what questions Ilya asked Max. She was American, after all, and he doubted she knew much about Russia or the war. She was visiting before all this broke out, and he couldn't blame her if she wanted nothing more but to go home. To get away from the deaths and killing. He continued pacing but kept his eyes planted on the car and finally, Ilya got out and strode toward the inn with Max trotting by his side.

Peter forced his gait to slow as he walked toward them. "Max, I am so glad you are safe."

She tilted her head and gave a small smile. "So am I." She turned to Ilya. "I'm free to go now?"

"Yes, but you will stay with my group. You are not to leave under any circumstances. You understand?"

"I understand."

Once Ilya left, Peter offered her his arm and they strolled down the street.

"What happened?"

"I got lost. The alcove I was watching from must have had a secret door because when I leant on the wall, I found myself in an entirely different ti... area."

"Where?"

"It doesn't matter now, but I tried to warn you about the trap. Did you hear me shout?"

"No. But as you saw, we had our own mighty defense arrive. I don't think the Bolsheviks saw that coming." He stopped and faced her, winding his arms around her. "And you are safe."

Max nodded. "I am. Is Karina?"

"Yes, she is well."

"Good."

Max looked at him then, and he couldn't help but lean into her sapphire eyes. "I was so worried about you." His gaze went to her mouth. Her lips opened slightly and she swallowed. He brought his lips down on hers and kissed her as if he would never get the chance again. He wanted to keep her within his arms forever.

Max's stomach rumbled, breaking the spell.

"Sorry," she said, her mouth still pressed against his.

Peter pulled back and laughed. She was beautiful, she was here, and she was hungry. "Come, you need a meal." Peter's own appetite came back with force.

※

Peter guided Max past the table where Elena was talking to her brother. Elena didn't look happy and Peter tried to hurry Max past, but too late, Kolya spotted them.

"Come. Come sit down," Kolya said, waving to the bench seat opposite him and Elena.

Elena huffed and placed her cup down on the table with a loud thunk. Without a word to Kolya or Peter and Max, she stormed off to the bar.

Kolya chuckled, watching Elena disappear into the crowd. "My sister is a hot-tempered thing, is she not?"

Peter grinned. "She is always in a mood about something or other."

Kolya left them to their meals and went in search of Elena.

Once they'd had their fill, Max yawned and sat back, her eyelids drooping. In another situation, Peter would think she looked seductive, but he knew it was because she was exhausted. He raised his hand and caught the eye of the owner.

"Could you show this woman to her room, please?"

"*Da*."

Peter let the warm wine wash down his throat, smiling inwardly. Max had agreed to come with him to the Black Sea if she couldn't find her guide or anyone from her group before then. She hadn't agreed to accompany him to Romania, saying her friends would be worried about her as she was for them. But it was a start. Peter would do all he could between now and when he and Karina sailed to change her mind.

"Ah, there you are," Vanya said, plunking down on the opposite bench and waving for the serving girl to bring him a cup of vodka. "I have spoken to Ilya. He and his trusted men are watching everyone closely. They know a spy is among us."

Peter nodded. "We were lucky to get Karina out of that trap. Thank the gods, Ilya sent Kolya. Surely whoever learned of the trap, would know who betrayed our mission."

"They have no idea. The intel came from someone already

embedded with the Bolsheviks. But whoever that is, they don't know who is reporting our movements to the Reds."

Peter drank the last of his wine. Vanya put up his arm to call for more.

"*Nyet*," Peter said. "It's time to sleep. I am to take Karina to Denmark, and we leave for the Black Sea and Romania tomorrow."

"I will come with you."

"Ilya said he will send a contingency with me. I don't know who he has chosen."

"I will speak with him. Have you thought about Max? She may be the spy in our fold."

"*Nyet*."

"She did go when the Bolsheviks attacked us. It doesn't look good."

"I don't believe that. She has explained what happened and I believe her." Peter stood up. "There is nothing more to be said."

CHAPTER 14

During the next few days, Max occupied herself tending to the horses. Ilya was waiting for his next orders and Peter spent most of his time with his general, working on the safest route to the Black Sea. She would have liked to be a part of those plans—she knew she could help with the stratagems if she had maps and the exact locations of enemy troops—but the soldiers were wary of her after her disappearance. She could understand that, but Max also knew Elena and her friends were talking up Max's disappearance, trying to convince the general and Peter that Max was a spy.

Max scoffed silently. If only Elena knew how much Ilya cared for Max. His reasons for keeping her out of the plans were because he hoped she would return home, and that was only because he feared for her safety there in Russia.

It wasn't all bad though—Peter spent most of his free time with her. One night, he taught her how to play Scat, the card game enjoyed by many of the soldiers. Needing three players, Peter talked Yegor into playing. Max would have preferred Vanya, but he was too busy flirting with every woman who came into the camp from the nearby village.

It took some time to become comfortable with the deck, thirty-two cards from the ace to sevens and instead of the normal suits, acorns, leaves, hearts, and bells. However, once she did, she enjoyed playing. The game was simple and once learned, Max won more times than she lost.

Yegor, though, hadn't seemed pleased with her quick learning. Max often had the feeling he watched her too closely, not as a man watched a woman, but as someone waiting for her to say or do something, he could call her out on.

After a card game, Max waited until they were alone in one of the private salons of the inn and asked Peter about his friend. "Doesn't Yegor like me?"

They sat on an old sofa before a smoldering fire drinking the last of the night's wine. Peter put his arm around her shoulders and pulled her into his side. "Of course, he does. If he seems distant it is most likely because he is missing his fiancée. She is in Kiev and he is trying to talk Ilya into letting him come with us to Odessa." He squeezed her shoulders. "With you here, he more than likely wishes she was also."

Max could understand him missing his fiancée, but that didn't calm her worries. He had definitely become cooler toward her lately.

"Are you tired?" Peter asked, angling his head and lifting her chin.

"Mmm." Max smiled at his gaze lingering on his lips as he spoke.

Before she knew it, he twisted his body so they were facing one another and began kissing her. All thoughts of Yegor and his imaginings disappeared as she indulged in the kiss, breathing in his man-soap scent, giving herself over to all the feelings. If she could crawl into his skin at that moment, she would have been a happy woman.

The passion ignited parts of her she didn't know existed. Shivers of excited sensuality ran down her back, her arms, her neck. Every part of her became alive and before she knew it, their hands were going in all directions, both trying to feel the other's skin. Whether Peter pushed her, or she pulled him, it didn't matter because all she wanted was him on top of her.

Somewhere in her mind, she knew she shouldn't be getting so close to someone from that time. She would have to leave him; she would have to go back to her own world. But another voice kept telling her, Abby and Izzy stayed in their beloveds' times.

Nothing mattered at that moment though. The only thing her clouded mind could take in were the pleasurable sensations the handsome Dane elicited and the need to be closer to Peter.

He had already opened Max's shirt when she tried to unbutton his shirt. She wanted to feel his skin on hers, wanted to quench both their thirsts, wanted to go all the way.

He kissed her mouth, face, neck, and was on his way along her jawline when he let out a groan. Max arched her back in answer, still trying to rid him of that blasted shirt.

He groaned again, his warm breath fanning over her neck, then he pulled back. Gazing dark-eyed and predatory, he closed his eyes and pulled her shirt together.

Sitting back, he rubbed his hands over his face. "I'm sorry, Max. I shouldn't have taken advantage of you like that."

Max pulled the sides of her shirt, one over the other, and stilled, slowly lowering her hands that a second before had grappled with his shirt, but now hung limply in midair. Confusion filled the spaces between the dissipating clouds in her mind. She sat up and buttoned her shirt. "Don't apologize. I was a willing partner. Why did you stop? Don't you want me?"

She had never been so honest before. She couldn't help it with Peter though. She had wanted him to make love to her, still wanted him to. Her nerves were taut; so too was her passion. She wanted release and here he was saying he didn't want to make love to her.

Peter dropped his hands and turned to her. "Want you? I have never wanted someone so much in all my life." His gaze, earnest and torn. "You are beautiful, but you deserve better than being made love to on a sofa in the middle of a war."

He stood up and bending, placed a kiss on the top of her head. "Good night, my love."

Then he left. Just like that. Left her there alone, her skin still tingling from his touch, her lips still desperate for his mouth on them.

Max sat there for she didn't know how long and fought to get her thoughts together. If they had been anywhere else, she knew he wouldn't have stopped. She was being stupid. Anyone could have walked in on them. It would have been embarrassing, and their impropriety could have hurt Peter's plans to get Karina to safety.

Max stood up and moved to the window. Late season snow fluttered down on the now white ground. It must have been late because she could see no footsteps or wheel tracks in the beautiful white blanket. In another time and place, she and Peter could be out there building a snowman or making snow angels. Max tried to imagine Peter laughing and having fun and of course, her mind went straight to the kisses they would delight in.

Again, she thought about how her sisters stayed with their beloveds.

She shook her head and turned away from the imaginary scene. She didn't really know Peter, she didn't know how he would react to playing in the snow, even if he would play in the snow at all. What he was like here in the middle of the Russian Revolution could be quite different to what he was like in his home country. Max didn't even know what he did in Denmark. She knew he was a count, but he told her most royals were counts and countesses these days. The royal family had no say in the governing of Denmark, and everyone pursued their own interests. But Max was too busy thinking about more kisses to ask what interests he pursued.

She made her way to her room thinking how little she knew of Peter and how much she missed Garrett and home. The room was small, but the smell of disinfectant told Max it was clean. Two beds, smaller than a normal single, were tucked away in the corners and they couldn't have looked more luxurious to Max than at that moment.

One of the beds already had a rucksack on it, so Max plopped down on the other. Wondering if her room companion was Elena or Karina, Max opened her backpack and withdrew her precious parcel. She unwrapped it and gazed at the orb. She'd been in Russia for over four weeks, nearly five if she counted correctly; how long had passed at home? She didn't think Garrett would haul her back again, not after what happened last time he did, but surely, he would have tried if she hadn't returned home after four weeks. She smashed her lips together. Of course, time wasn't passing the same for Garrett and Bree—for them she might have only been gone for a day or two.

She started wrapping the orb up just as Elena walked into the room.

"What is that?" Elena asked, pointing to the orb.

Max smiled and tucked it back into her backpack. "It's just a family trinket, something I always carry with me." She tied up the pack. "It reminds me of home."

Elena's eyes narrowed but she didn't say any more about

it; instead, she sat down on her bed with a loud sigh. "Home. You have family?"

"Yes. Do you have more family than your brother?"

"*Nyet*. Only my brother survives."

"I'm sorry. I lost my parents a year or so ago." Elena looked up at that, her eyes filled with sadness. Max smiled. "I still think I hear their voices, especially if I've done something they wouldn't approve of. Do you?"

"*Da,* but I hope what I do will make them proud."

"I think we always want our parents to be proud of us."

"*Da*." Elena kept her coat on and climbed under the scarce covers. "I miss them."

"Me too."

"How did your parents die?" Elena asked.

"They were in a car accident. Another car came from out of nowhere and collided with theirs."

"Oh, how terrible. What car did they drive?"

Max frowned. Elena seemed to have risen from her grief over her own parents' death at the mention of cars. "Um, I think it was a Model T Ford." Max was pretty sure that model was around in 1917.

"Yes, I've seen them in pictures, the black ones. I've only driven a Fiat truck, I would like a nice car."

"Perhaps after the wars are over, you will have the chance. If you don't mind saying, how did your parents die?"

Her face fell in sadness again. "My mother died when I was eight years old and my father was all but murdered, thrown out of the house where he worked and left on the streets in the middle of severe winter with what little money he had, no food and only the clothes on his back. That was ten years ago now; my brother and I have looked after one another ever since."

"That's awful. Why was your father thrown out of his house?"

"Not his house, the house where he worked. Father was the gardener and my brother helped him keep a wonderful garden. The young prince accused my father of stealing vegetables, of selling them at the marketplace for his own benefit." She eyed Max. "He didn't, the prince did. He and his friends took the vegetables, sold them, and did who knows what with the money. My brother tried to tell the duchess, but she wouldn't hear a word against her beloved son. She ousted both my brother and father that very moment."

"What did you do?"

"I had been sent to my uncle's house in Kuban only two weeks before, and it was a month later that my brother finally arrived to tell us what had happened and asked my uncle to help my father. My uncle took us to find my father but when he wasn't where my brother had left him, my uncle went to the duchess's house. It was the cook of the house; she told my uncle what happened, and she also told him my father was found dead in an alley not far from the house a week later. The cook said he was murdered for his belongings, but my brother said he had no belongings. My brother told me about the prince and the vegetables—he knew the prince was the guilty one."

Elena sat up and glared at Max with wet eyes. "The duchess murdered him; she knew my father would never survive the winter without work."

Max didn't know what to say. Her heart ached for the young Elena, who would have only been fifteen or sixteen at the time.

"I'm sorry," Max said.

Flopping back on the bed, Elena let out a loud huff and rolled over to face the wall. "I am tired."

Max sat watching Elena's back; from the way it convulsed every now and then, she could tell the woman was crying but trying not to let Max know.

Turning off the light, Max climbed under her covers.

As she fell asleep, Max decided she would see Peter and Karina safely on a ship to England, then she would return home. She missed Garrett and Bree and she promised Garrett she would come back. Maybe if she opened herself up to the possibility, she could meet someone in her time. But her last thought was, *there is no one in any time like Peter*.

CHAPTER 15

The next morning, Peter spied Max talking with Ilya again. He frowned. If they had only met the night Peter brought the lost American to camp, surely, they would still be strangers. He caught himself then and gave a wry smile. He didn't feel like he and Max were strangers; why would he think they should be? Some people render others at ease from the very beginning of their relationship, and where he could see Max doing so, Ilya wasn't someone Peter thought anyone would warm to, especially not immediately. However, he was now becoming increasingly curious as to what they could possibly have to talk about.

"Peter."

He turned at Karina's voice.

"I was hoping to speak before we left. Did you know Ilya has had orders to free the Romanovs? He is leaving today, and I want to go with him. He said he would try to free my grandmother also."

"No. No, Karina. It is too dangerous. The Bolsheviks will be looking for you and I am certain they were not pleased to lose you to the Whites. We must leave Russia."

She stuck her small chin up. "*Nyet*. I am Russian and I want to fight for my country. I cannot leave my grandmother to whatever fate the Bolsheviks have in store for her. She needs me and I am of age. You have no say in the affairs of a princess, Count Peter."

Peter nearly spat. Of age. She was sixteen years old. Just out of nursery school. And the way she said "Count Peter," as if he should be bowing to her instead of saving her life.

"Princess, I am your cousin and I have been allotted the pleasure of saving your life and I have done that. I will not see my work undone, and your father is expecting you to return to Denmark."

She pouted at the mention of her father. "He did not want my presence before the war, why should he want it now?"

"He was grieving, child. He—"

"So was I."

Tears fell down her cheeks and Peter was undone. He took her into his arms, and she sobbed into his shoulder.

Not knowing what else to do, he patted her back. "I know. Shhh, everything will be all right."

Karina was twelve years old when she was sent to live with her grandmother, Grand Duchess Anericka, and as such she was a princess in Russia. He could understand a girl of her age preferring the role of a princess to a countess, but being a princess in Russia was no longer safe. She would be killed for her royal ties and Peter could not contend with that.

She squirmed out of his arms and gave him a defiant look. "I will stay and fight for my Russia, for my Russian family."

"*Nyet*. You will come with me to the Black Sea where we will board a ship for England. Now after such a long voyage, we will stay for a time in England but then we will travel to Denmark, where you will rejoin your family and live a long, happy life."

He must have talked for too long because Karina had lost

interest in his words and had her focus firmly planted on Ilya and Max.

"I wonder what they are talking about. Did you see Ilya laugh? He seems content in her company."

Peter glared at the two of them, seemingly so comfortable in one another's company. Max looked over and her smile vanished at Peter's hostile stare. Good, thought Peter. He didn't like her being so friendly with a man like Ilya. He was a handsome and powerful man, and Peter considered himself neither of those things.

Ilya glanced in the direction Max looked and then leaned forward and whispered something to her. She laughed. Ilya hugged her and strode toward his men.

Max walked up to Peter and Karina. "Don't you two have anything better to do than watch me and Ilya?"

"What were you doing with him?" Peter wanted to know.

"I was talking to him, is that okay? I didn't think it would be disallowed. After all, I am here because of his welcome."

"He is a very nice man," Karina said.

With the strange look in his cousin's eye as she watched Ilya, Peter was glad she was leaving with him.

Max smiled and Peter knew then she saw Karina's fascination with the general as well.

"Yeah, very nice. So, what are you two up to? Are we heading out today too?"

"I want to stay with Ilya and save my grandmother, but Peter is being extremely mean."

"I am to take you home, Karina, and Denmark is your home. You were born there; do you not remember?"

"I remember, but Russia has been my home since I was but twelve years old. She is my country now."

"Don't you miss your father?" Max asked.

The sadness returned to her eyes, pushing away her rebellion. "No."

Max took her hands. "I don't believe you. Uh-uh, don't say anything you might regret. Come on, and I'll help you pack." She narrowed her eyes at Peter. "We are moving out today, aren't we?"

"Yes."

A voice grated beside Peter. "When do we leave?"

Peter jumped at the sound of Vanya's voice. He hadn't even noticed the man had moved to his side. "What? Oh, noon at the latest. Are you coming?"

"*Da*, Yegor, me and Elena. Do not look so distraught. We have a small troop also."

"How many?"

"Five."

Peter quickly added himself and Max to the number. "That makes ten fighters in all. Less than I was hoping for, but perhaps better for sneaking around the country."

"*Da*, but I make it nine unless you are counting Karina as a fighter."

"*Nyet*. Max is coming as far as the Black Sea with us."

"Interesting." Vanya grinned. "And you will say goodbye to her there?"

"She will be going back to America, so yes we will say our goodbyes there."

"Interesting." With that, Vanya marched to the vehicle where Ilya stood.

Peter rubbed his chin. He wasn't looking forward to saying goodbye to Max. He liked having her around and he liked her kisses. Yes, he would miss both very much.

He shook the thought out of his mind and refocused on Vanya, hoping he asked Ilya for a tank. One of the French light tanks would have been appreciated.

Once Ilya and his company moved out, there were only three armored cars left and Peter assigned the drivers and passengers to each in his mind. Two were like the previous ones he had driven in and sat three, and one could fit five. It would be tight but better than walking.

Vanya and Yegor stood next to Peter. "What are you thinking?" Vanya asked.

"That there is no tank."

"*Nyet*," Yegor said. "And Ilya has people ready to collect these cars in Mykolaiv, and he says we must go the rest of the way by foot. The roads are becoming increasingly cluttered with Reds."

"That might be so, but Mykolaiv is around one hundred and thirty kilometers from Odessa."

"Perhaps we can find other vehicles in Mykolaiv or close by."

"I hope so because even at a forced march, that would take us nearly thirty hours of walking."

"No need to worry, Peteor, we will find a way."

Peter nodded. He trusted Ilya's reasoning for reclaiming the vehicles even if he didn't trust his relationship with Max. "Yegor, you take the gun on the second vehicle and choose the best gunner for the first. Split the other four soldiers between the cars. Vanya, you will drive the third car with the rest of us."

Vanya nodded. "Who will take the gun?"

"I will."

Karina and Elena were talking in hushed tones a little way from the third car and once Elena climbed into the vehicle, Karina hurried to Peter's side.

"Peter, can I have a word with you before we leave?"

"What is it?" He grimaced. As if he didn't know.

"I am worried about Maxine. Elena said she saw her with some sort of communication device and believes her to be a spy."

"What sort of communication device, and why didn't she report to me?"

"She doesn't think you will believe her. She says you are too infatuated with the American and cannot see past your manly needs."

Peter laughed at that. His manly needs? Did she think him such a Neanderthal that he could not think? He frowned. His feelings for Max had taken over his thoughts of late. Had he been neglecting his duty to Karina? He could not think Max would be a spy, but she could be an informant to the Americans. He must not lower his wariness with any concerned on the mission, and he must be on the alert for any wrongdoings.

"What did it look like and where is she keeping it?"

"It's a hard egg-like thing and she keeps it in her backpack."

"Don't say anything to anyone else and tell Elena to leave it to me."

CHAPTER 16

Hearing the cars motors start up outside the inn, Max made her way out to the cars. Elena leaned against a car, talking to Kolya

By the time Max found Peter, Karina was with him. He glanced in her direction and his face froze out all expression.

Now what had she done? Maybe Ilya was right; maybe she should just go home. They probably didn't need her help, probably didn't even want it, but Max had a feeling they would be glad she was there if something went wrong. She also had a feeling something wasn't right about Elena and after their conversation about families, Max felt sorry for her, but the woman's continued coldness soon put paid to that.

Of course, there was the fact that Elena had a thing for Peter and was super jealous of Max. There was something fishy about the way she pushed so hard to make everyone believe Max was the spy in their midst.

She sucked in her bottom lip. Someone had been responsible for the trap in Kharkov.

The thought that Elena might be trying to deflect suspicion away from herself crossed Max's mind. But she swept it away. No matter how rotten Elena might be, she wouldn't endanger Peter. It was clear to anyone who looked at her: the woman was in love with him. No, she was just worried about the newcomer and in her shoes, Max would be too.

Max took a step but hesitated. What had Karina said that made him so stony faced? She snorted. She was just being paranoid. It probably had nothing to do with her and anyway, it wasn't as if she was stuck there, not like Abby was in Scotland past. She had the orb and could go home anytime she wanted.

By the time she got to Peter, Karina had left and climbed into the largest car with Elena.

"Hi, what's going on?"

"Ilya has left us with three cars and eight soldiers, and we leave now."

"Elena is one of the soldiers?"

"Yes."

"And me?"

Peter smiled. "Yes, and that makes nine soldiers and myself to protect Karina and take her safely to a ship."

"We can do it. Actually, it's probably better not to have a full battalion traipsing through Russia. Three cars are easier to handle if we have to run."

Peter's admiring gaze turned to her. "That's what I thought also."

She tried not to blush. All thought of his stony face went out of her mind, and she teetered toward his smile but straightened at the last minute. "Where am I to go then?"

"You will travel in the third car. Come."

"Will it fit all of us?"

He nodded and helped her into the front seat beside Vanya, who was driving. Karina and Elena were in the back. Peter climbed up on the gunner's seat but bent over Max's shoulder.

"There's room up here if you need air during the drive."

Max glanced at Elena's black expression. "Thanks, I might take you up on that."

"Me too," Elena said. "I do not like being in the back seat. I will need fresh air too."

"Sure." Peter pulled his head back and popped it through the portal.

Max half turned in her seat as Vanya got under way and looked at Elena. "I thought you'd stay with Ilya."

"I wanted to help Karina and Ilya agreed I should. Do you have a problem?"

"No way, I just thought you'd stay with the main army is all. Are you excited to be going home, Karina?"

"*Nyet*. I want to stay here and fight for Russia, for my family, but Peter is stubborn man."

"He's risked a lot to save you. You know he cares for you deeply."

"*Da,* he is like big brother, but I am not little girl."

Elena let out a snort at that.

"I am not a little girl, Elena. I am of age and if I can marry and make babies, I can fight for my country."

Max tried not to look startled at that, but her eyes widened anyway. "But you're only sixteen, aren't you?"

"*Da*, and when I return home, I will be made to meet eligible bachelors just like any other debutante." She screwed up her nose. "But I will not like any of them—my heart is Russian, and I want to marry a Russian even if he is not a noble." Her eyes flickered. "So long as he is wealthy, of course."

Max laughed. "Of course."

She settled back into her seat and gazed out at the passing landscape. It was beautiful. Untouched fields of snowy white. She couldn't see any animal or human tracks. The trees in the distance sported thick snow hats, but the lower branches were speckled green and white. The snow mustn't have been too thick on the road or Max supposed they wouldn't be driving through it, but looking at it, she thought it could be feet deep in some places.

As they neared the forest, something black moved. Max nudged Vanya in the side and pointed ahead. "What's that?"

He squinted and leant forward over the steering wheel. The black thing leapt onto all fours and clumped through the snow to a small thicket.

Vanya chuckled. "A bear." The car trundled past and he pointed a fist out Max's side window. "See? She has babies."

Two, no, three little brown puffs bounced through the snow to meet their mother. "Aw," Max cooed as she plastered her nose on the window. "They're so cute."

"You not say that if you meet old one."

"They are dangerous," Elena said. "Peter. Peter."

Peter ducked his head down and raised his brows.

"Shoot the bear. There." She poked her finger in the air at the bear and her cubs.

"No," Max said. "They aren't doing anything to you. Why would you kill them?"

"They are dangerous," she said again. As if that was all she had to say about it to get her way.

"*Nyet*," Peter said and went back to his position.

Max heard Elena's back bang against her seat and even the huff she exhaled, but thankfully she didn't say any more about the bears. Instead, she complained about her comfort and pushed Vanya in the back. "Why are there no cushions? Surely someone could have brought cushions. This seat is hard as a stone."

"Why didn't you?" Vanya asked.

"It's not that bad, Elena," Karina said. "Do you want to change places?"

"*Nyet*. Peter? Can I come up there with you?"

Peter called down. "Not until we are fully in the forest."

Max couldn't help rolling her eyes slowly up at the roof of the car at Elena's antics and caught Vanya's gaze just as she'd finished. He laughed and nodded vigorously.

"What is funny?" Karina asked.

Max joined in his laughter. "Nothing," she spluttered. "Stop it, Vanya. You must be tired."

"*Nyet*. Not tired. Happy is all."

Elena's snarl had Max turning to the back.

Elena narrowed her eyes. "I'm glad you're happy, Vanya, because I am not."

"*Nyet*, is good he is happy, is it not?" Karina said.

"If you say so, Princess."

Karina smiled but Max frowned. The girl was such an innocent she didn't even hear the bitterness in Elena's voice when she called her princess. A shiver ran down Max's spine. The woman didn't like royals? Of course, Max knew she blamed the duchess and the prince for her parents' deaths, but it hadn't occurred to her that Elena might think all royals were that mean. What the blazes was she doing fighting for them then?

Vanya must have missed the exchange because he was still chuckling to himself.

Max sat back once more and gazed at the passing trees and shrubs. She would talk to Vanya later. Maybe he could shed some light on Elena's actions.

They drove in silence until Elena managed to rise high enough to grab the rim of the portal and, pulling herself up, she plonked in Peter's lap. Peter let out a raspy puff of air but didn't push her away.

"It is nice, *da?*" Elena said.

"*Da*," Peter said.

Max folded her arms over her chest and gazed out the

windscreen. He could have told Elena to sit back down; he didn't have to let her sit on him. The emotions roiling around her body were alien to her. Why her chest would hurt was beyond her, and her stomach felt sick. She rubbed her forehead. It was hot. Was she coming down with some sort of flu? What if it was bacterial? Did they even have antibiotics in 1917?

Peter's voice floated down into the car's cabin. "Time to go back down."

"*Nyet*, not yet," Elena said.

"Now, we are coming out of the forest."

Elena let out a loud expulsion of air. She squirmed down onto her seat. "It was nice up there."

Max shivered and turned to Vanya. "Is there a heater in here?"

"*Da*, it on."

"Really?" It didn't feel like the car was heated. She gazed at the snow-covered fields. Maybe it was warmer in the car than out, but it couldn't have been by much.

The hours passed and other than hushed conversations every now and then between Elena and Karina, while Max or Vanya pointed out sights either she wanted to know about or he told her about of his own accord, the car silently made its way through the countryside. Max usually fell asleep on long road trips, but she couldn't stop gazing at the sights around her. The tall snow-covered mountains in the distance, fields, some still spotted white with snow with green grass fighting to feel the sunlight on their blades, forests of pines. The raw beauty of Russia had Max in awe.

The sun had long gone down by the time they pulled up at a tiny inn on the outskirts of a small-town Vanya said was Poltava.

They drove along narrow dirt roads that were more like lanes, past small and large wooden houses, and stopped at a four-floor wooden building decorated in yellow and green ochre.

The hotel was quaint and although Max was freezing in the car and even colder once out of it, she relaxed in the warmth of the hotel the moment she stepped over the threshold. It was busy with people going in all directions throughout the maze of doors. Vanya spoke to the man behind the counter, and he plucked some keys off the board and guided them to their rooms.

Max's room was clean and while small, it was still thankfully received. She didn't even mind having to freshen up in the communal bathroom and by the time she sat down to a hearty dinner of stew and fresh bread, she was feeling hungry but content.

As soon as she was able, Max left the dining room and made her way to the sitting room and the wonderful fire. Glad it had only a couple of other people there, she sat down on the sofa and let the warmth from the flames cover her. It wasn't long before she could take off her gloves. She wriggled her fingers in front of the fire and sighed. That felt so good. She wasn't sure if she would ever get feeling back into her hands.

"Nice fire," Peter said as he sat down next to her.

She immediately stiffened. "It is."

"I'm sorry, would you prefer I didn't sit here?"

"What? No, you can sit there, it's a free country."

Sadness washed over his face. "Not so free anymore."

Max's heart went out to him. She should be more careful with sprouting silly sayings before thinking. The country wasn't free, and it probably never would be.

"What about Denmark? Is it free?"

"Free from dictatorships. Yes, we are a free and lucky country."

"You're a count. Isn't that royalty?"

"I have royal connections, but in Denmark, if a prince or princess marries without the monarch's consent, they and their heirs relinquish the titles, and all become counts and countesses. Karina's father and my father did so for love. And we do not adhere to royalty conventions like Russia or England do. Our government rules the country and being a democratic state, each level of government is voted for by the people, so in effect, the people rule Denmark. As it is for the United States, yes?"

"Yes. But voting isn't compulsory, so perhaps we have gone too far in our bid for complete freedom. I mean, the only people who vote are passionate about the policies of one side or the other of the parties."

"That is a problem for all countries who don't have compulsory voting, I'm afraid."

Max wondered about his speech; he obviously had a good education. "Do you live on family money or do you have a job?"

He laughed. "I work, yes. I run the family company, engineering is my trade."

"Ooh, nice. Do you build stuff?"

He chuckled. "Well not on my own or with my own hands, but yes, we build bridges, buildings, things like that." He gazed into her eyes with genuine interest. "But tell me about your country from your eyes. Do you have family there?"

Max wanted to hear more about his work and family, but she said, "Two sisters, a brother and a cousin. Although now that my sisters are married and have their own lives away from the family home, I feel a bit out of sorts there. It just feels dull and empty now."

"No parents?"

"No, they died in a horrible accident."

He took her hand in his but didn't say anything. Maybe he

didn't know what to say; maybe he'd never lost someone close to him before.

"What about your family?" Max asked. "How many are there?"

"My parents and of course my uncle and Karina. We have other cousins." He laughed. "Many, in fact, too many to count."

"Sounds hectic."

"It can be. Perhaps you will travel to Denmark and meet my family. The country has beautiful landscapes." He gazed blankly, a wistful expression on his face as if picturing his country in his mind. "Our mountains are majestic, and our lakes are clean and fresh, the most wonderful teal color. The green comes from the melting snow flowing in from the mountains, and the blue tinge comes from the clear blue sky above."

Max felt his love for his homeland and smiled. "Sounds lovely."

"It is, and I would like to show my country to you before you go back to America. I am certain you would love it as I do."

Had he just asked if Max would go home with him? "Are you inviting me along?"

He shrugged as if it meant nothing. "If it is something you would desire, you are most welcome to travel with me and Karina."

He stood up and held his hand out. "Let me walk you to your room. It is unsafe for a woman alone."

Max gazed into his eyes. He appeared uncertain. Maybe he hadn't meant to invite her but once he had, he worried she wouldn't want to visit his homeland. Of course, she would love to, but perhaps they both knew once at the port, they had to go their separate ways. But that was then, and this was now. She took his hand. "Sure."

Once she was on her feet, he let her hand go and opened the door, to let her pass through first. Once Max passed, she waited—the hallway was wide enough that they could walk side by side.

Peter didn't say a word as they walked to the door of her room and stopped there. Max gazed up into Peter's eyes and said quietly, "I guess it's good night then."

"Yes." His voice was gruff and his eyes intent. He cleared his throat. "Good night, Maxine."

They stood gazing into one another's eyes, then Peter let go of her hand and took her into his arms, kissing her deeply. She wrapped her arms around his neck and kissed him, letting her mind and body fill only with the sensation of their lips pressed together.

Peter finished the kiss and drew back, his eyes filled with passion and his breath shallow and fast. "Good night, Maxine."

He untangled her arms from around his neck, quickly turned and strode down the hall while Max leaned her back against the door and sighed. After the thrumming through her body eased, she turned and retreated into her room.

CHAPTER 17

The second day was long and tiring, and after twelve hours cooped up in the car, they finally found an inn to spend the night. Vanya said they made good time though and had travelled at least one hundred and eighty kilometers.

Max was disappointed at not having time to spend alone with Peter but was also thankful for the bed that night.

The next day, they had only traveled for about eight hours before Yegor's car got a flat tire. By the time it was repaired, it was dark and it took three hours more to find an inn to spend the night.

Again, everyone was too exhausted to do more than eat a late supper and go to bed, but Max found it hard to sleep. Her thoughts filled with Peter and the memories of their kisses, and her body warmed all over at the remembrance of every sensation his lips brought.

Her logical brain knew it was probably for the best; after all, she would have to leave him at some point, but her heart and every cell of her body hoped they would get the chance to be alone again, to kiss again.

Day four, they were up early and ready to continue their journey. Max was glad they hadn't come upon any Reds and except for the flat tire, their travelling had no real incidents. She stepped out into the gloomy morning light and hoped it would be another day free of conflict.

As the car meandered along the road through the countryside, Max was still enthralled with the scenery. Russia was the most beautiful country she had ever visited and as soon as she could, she would return and retrace the route this journey was taking her. It would be fun to see how everything had changed in her time.

Distant gunshots startled Max out of her ruminations. "Vanya?"

"There's fighting ahead," Peter called down. "Vanya, stop the car and tell Yegor and Dima to do the same."

The cars stopped and the soldiers clambered out. Max was out of the car the moment it stopped and looking over the bonnet down the hill, she gawped at the battle. The Reds in their khaki issued uniforms seemed to be winning against the haphazardly dressed White volunteers. Although the Whites retreated a little with every flurry of gunshots, the Reds being on higher ground descended and closed the gap.

But from behind another hill, an army of Whites joined their comrades, and then it was the Reds that retreated quickly behind a more distant rise.

Yegor pointed. "They have a Mark V tank."

Peter said, "Our troops haven't got a chance against that."

Max scanned the area. The tank was off to the side closest to their position and the rest of the Red Army were shooting over a rise at the Whites. "No one is guarding the tank," she said. "Do you have grenades?"

They all looked at her as if she'd lost her mind.

"What?"

"We have grenades," Vanya said. "What are you thinking?"

"We go down there and plant some in the tank. Without it, the sides are more or less equal, and the Whites can win this battle."

Peter frowned at her. "Karina is our first priority." He pointed away from the road. "We'll go that way and skirt behind our army, coming back to the road some miles away."

Vanya shook his head. "*Nyet*, Peteor. The snow is deep at the bottom of the hill, we will be stuck and Karina will be in more danger."

"What do you suggest?" Peter asked.

Vanya looked at Peter and Max. "I think Maxine is right. Without the tank, our army will succeed," Vanya said and pulled his bag out of the vehicle. "The grenades."

Peter looked at the bag and snorted. "All right."

Vanya began clipping grenades to his belt.

"Nyet." Peter's gaze rested on Karina for a moment before he said, "I will not send someone else; I am in command, I will go." He narrowed his eyes at Vanya. "You will protect Karina with your life, *da*?"

Vanya nodded and gave Peter his grenades, which he proceeded to slip to his belt.

"Give me some," Max said.

Peter shook his head. "You will stay here. Yegor, you stay too. We'll need to get these cars out with Karina fast if all hell breaks loose."

Karina and Elena emerged from the car.

Peter rounded on her. "Get Karina back into the car, you too, Vanya, and be ready to move out at my command. Yegor, take the gun."

Elena hustled Karina back into the car.

"Dima, have your car ready." Peter put the last grenade in its pouch and said, "Pasha and Feliks, follow me."

Max scowled at their backs as they slid silently down the hill toward the back of the tank. The men did as they were ordered and while Yegor slipped his lean body through the hatch to take his position at the gun, Max swallowed down her ire. She wasn't one of his men and he couldn't order her around. Vanya took his bag off his shoulder so he could slide into the driver's seat. Without thinking, Max grabbed the bag and ran after Peter. She glanced back, hoping Vanya wouldn't shout out and have the Red Army descend upon them. But other than a rude gesture with his hand, he kept quiet.

Max fell flat on her back and hugged the bag to her chest so as not to slow her down, then let gravity pull her quickly down the hill. To her right, she could see the Reds lining the rise in the distance. Gun blasts echoed through the air. She was used to hearing such noise in training, but knowing the bullets were meant to kill, her heart raced more with each blast. Out of the mayhem three soldiers sprinted toward the tank.

She slid right up to Peter, who glared at her.

He grated a whisper. "Get back."

Max shook her head and putting her finger against her lips to keep him silent, she pointed to the battle. Peter and the other two soldiers looked where she pointed. The soldiers were getting closer.

"They mean to take the tank," Peter grated.

Max nodded and plucked a grenade out of the bag. Staying low, she crept to the back of the tank with Peter close behind. Max wondered if the Whites were pushing the Reds back more because the blasts sounded like they were getting closer, making her heart race and throb in her temples.

Max clasped her shaking hands together to indicate a foot holder, hoping Peter understood what she wanted him to do. He sighed and did what she asked. She placed a foot in his hands, took in a deep breath, and leapt up to the top of the tank.

Peter and his men had their guns at the ready and Max

hoped they wouldn't have to use them. The hatch was closed but not locked into position. She pulled the pin on the grenade and carefully lifted the hatch. It screeched like a cat as it spun around, and her heart faltered but she held on for her life, trying not to drop the now live grenade. Getting a foothold on a weld joint, she held her breath, pulled the hatch open and tossed the grenade in. She immediately let go and slid off the back of the tank and onto the head of a person. They both fell to the ground and Max realized he was an enemy soldier, but she didn't have time to put her training into use before he shot his handgun and Max cried out as pain sliced through her leg. The grenade exploding in the tank rumbled through her body just as Peter pulled her off the soldier.

"Max."

She squinted at him; the sun shining behind formed a halo of light around his head and he looked like an angel. But another thought broke through: the injury couldn't have been too bad if it hurt so much. If it was worse, her own natural anesthesia would have come into play. She groaned and held her leg, wishing it was worse.

The White soldiers held their guns at the man, and one said something in Russian.

"*Nyet*," was his reply.

More gunshots sounded and the blasts sounded like they were getting closer. Max's heart raced faster than ever. She twisted around and poked her head around the tank. About three Reds were running their way. More shots sounded above them. Vanya and the other soldier had driven their cars down the hill and were now in firefights with the remaining Reds.

Peter said something in Russian to his men and pushed Max between the tank treads. "Stay here."

She nodded. It wasn't as if she could do anything else at

that moment. He gave her a hard, intent gaze then jumped up onto his feet.

The fighting didn't last long after that. Peter's group met up with the Whites and soon had the Reds in retreat. Most got away but about a dozen prisoners were taken. The leader of the Whites organized the injured to be ferried to field hospitals, and the rest were taken into custody.

Max refused to go to the hospital.

Peter helped Max to the car. "Commander Yudinich has offered us his camp for the night. You will see the doctor there."

Max was enjoying the feeling of his arm around her. "Don't worry about it, it's just a scrape."

He pulled her closer into his side. "I wasn't asking if you wanted to see one, I said you will see a doctor. That's an order."

She squirmed out of his arm and stood with her hands on her hips. "I don't take orders from you. I can look after myself, I don't need any doctors."

Of this time, she added silently. It wasn't a bad injury and the only thing to worry about was infection. She knew what to look for but if she kept it clean, she didn't think that would be a problem. Even if it was, did they have antibiotics there?

She pulled away from him, but he wrapped his arm around her waist and half carried her to the car. She tried to glare at him in contempt, but the brute ignored her.

They approached the car and Peter almost pushed Max inside. "You're going to the doctor now. Vanya, go directly to the field hospital."

Max bit her lip against the pain in her leg. No, it wasn't a severe injury, but it did hurt, and she hated not being able to walk by herself.

Once the car stopped, Peter lifted her out but didn't put her down. "I can walk, you know."

"I know."

And with that he carried her into a large tent and put her on a bed.

"Stay here." He left and Max figured he went to find a doctor.

Nurses scrambled about going from bed to bed, and in their efforts to triage the injured, helped the patients either sit or lie more comfortably. Every now and then one of the nurses would call out the Russian word, *"Vot!"*

And a doctor would appear out of nowhere to quickly examine the patient the nurse stood beside. He then either left them in the nurse's care or had soldiers wheel the bed into a privately partitioned part of the tent.

Max felt foolish for even being there. The men and women around her needed doctors, she didn't. She started to climb off the trolley and as her feet touched the ground, Peter emerged out of the chaos. He sat her back on the bed.

"Stay."

Max widened her eyes at him. "I'm not a dog."

He cocked his head as if unsure what she was saying.

"I'm fine. Let's go. The doctors and nurses have enough on their hands without me."

A doctor moved to Peter's side. "Let me be the judge of that."

Max was surprised at the English accent. "You're British?"

"Yes."

He proceeded to rip the leg of Max's trousers apart right up to the top of her thigh to better see the wound. While the nurse wheeled a small table next to the bed, Max noted two bowls, a pair of large tweezers and a plate of small cloth squares. Max also noted Peter seemed to try to look anywhere else but at her leg. She hid a smile, reveling in his discomfort. How would he react to women's clothing, or lack thereof, in her time?

The doctor stood back while the nurse cleaned the wound. When she'd finished, she hurried away into the throng of patients and medical staff. The doctor wiped a clean cloth over Max's injury.

"See? It's nothing," Max said.

"There is always a risk of infection."

"But if I keep it clean, it'll be fine."

"True."

The nurse returned with a bandage.

"Doris here will dress the wound and then you are free to leave."

"Thanks, Doc."

He smiled and frowned at the same time. "My pleasure."

Another nurse called out *"Vot"* from somewhere in the tent and the doctor rushed in the direction of her voice.

"What does *vot* mean?" Max asked Peter.

"Here. It lets the doctors know where to attend."

Once bandaged and feeling better about her injury, Max let Peter help her to the tent a soldier pointed them to as they emerged from the medical tent.

"From now on, you are to stay in the car no matter what happens, do you hear me?"

"I hear you but as I told you before, you can't order me around like the others. Do you *hear* me?"

"If you are to travel with us, you will obey me. It is for your own good, Max. Why do you fight with me?"

"Because I can help, that's why."

"You are too impulsive. You will end up getting yourself and anyone around you killed."

"Gee, thanks for that." She tried to sound as sarcastic as she could. "If you remember, I saved Yegor. And Andrei trusted me to carry a gun and although I didn't take it, I know how to use it. Why are you fighting with me?"

He looked over her shoulder into the distance. His eyes

held something she hadn't seen before. Fear? Anyone would be scared in the middle of a war, and Peter wouldn't be an exception there. And Max understood, he was also scared for his cousin's life, but he hadn't shown even a smidgeon of that fear before that moment.

When his gaze washed over her and rested on her bandaged leg, she knew in an instant it wasn't himself, or his men, or even his cousin, he was scared for. It was her.

Without thinking, she threw her arms around his neck and hugged him. He stiffened. She backed off but his hands on her back held her in place for a brief moment before letting go.

She gazed up into his eyes and her heart quickened at the emotion she saw there. Need, fear, passion, worry all rolled into one. She tried to make her voice light. "Hey, we got that tank together, didn't we?" He gave a small nod. "Well? See? My injury will heal, and we'll all have a better chance of surviving the mission if we fight together."

He pierced her with a hard gaze, then turned and strode away.

Max's racing heart ached without his touch and she ducked into the tent.

Glad no one else was there, and with her shaky legs unable to hold her upright any longer, Max collapsed onto the floor, and waited for her body to stop trembling and her heart to slow down.

Regaining control of her limbs, she crawled to the bed and hauled herself on it, sitting on the edge. She exhaled loudly. All she wanted was for him to take her into his arms and kiss her again, come inside the tent and spend the night with her, but for some reason he seemed so cold, not at all like the Peter who had walked her to her room that first night on the road. The way he'd kissed her then, she'd just assumed if the chance came up, he would like nothing better than to kiss her again. She sighed. But something had changed his mind about her. Somewhere in her thick brain she knew it was for the best, but that didn't stop her body and heart from wanting him.

Pulling her pack to her, she plunged her hand inside. Maybe it was better that Peter didn't try to get closer to her. After all, she shouldn't be there, they should have never met, and she shouldn't be fighting the Reds, trying to save a young woman from certain death. The realization of how close she came to being fatally injured dawned on her. What if she'd gotten herself killed, what would the history books make of that? She pulled the orb out and unwrapped it. Maybe she should just go home.

Peter's image, his emotion-filled eyes swam through her mind. He liked her, no, more than liked, he wouldn't be so worried she'd be hurt if it was only like.

Resting her hand on the top of the orb, the thought of Peter being hurt or even killed had her heart aching. No. She would stay and help as much as she could until Peter and Karina were safely on the ship.

She kissed the orb and at that moment Elena walked into the tent. Max stared at her, and Elena's gaze was firmly planted on the orb.

Blast. Not again. Elena's eyes brightened and she glared at Max. Max clumsily rewrapped the orb, saying, "Elena."

But Elena, smirk firmly on her face, rushed out of the tent before Max could say any more.

"Uh-oh." Max screwed up her nose. Had Elena decided the orb wasn't a family heirloom after all? She never really saw it properly the first time, but she got a good look this time. Whatever the woman thought would probably bite Max big time.

CHAPTER 18

Peter strolled to his tent, trying to make sense of the emotions swirling through his body. There was no doubt he was drawn to Max, but why? She wasn't like any woman he'd met before. In fact, unlike the women in Denmark or even England and Russia, she enjoyed fighting with her hands but didn't like using guns. Her eyes lit with excitement when he hoisted her to the top of the tank, but he noted a flicker of fear there as well. She appeared to like the adrenaline rush of danger.

His thoughts went to Denmark, where he headed up the family's construction business. Building apartment buildings, bridges and theaters weren't exactly adrenaline-inducing pursuits. He chuckled. A picture of him and Max traversing the scaffolding twenty stories up emerged in his mind. He supposed excitement could be found in his work but quickly deduced that sort of thing was never going to happen—he preferred to keep his feet firmly planted on the ground. Even with his Cossack blood, handling a boardroom of different personalities and opinions was excitement enough for him.

Or at least it had been—until he accepted the mission to

rescue his cousin—until he entered Russia—until he fought alongside his father's people—until he met Max.

But when he had thought about his life, the family he would build, he had always thought to meet a nice Dane, settle down and raise a family. Now he was confused. What did he want? Would he go to America if that was where Max went? His father left his Cossack family, his people, for Peter's mother. Could *he* leave Denmark, his family, his work?

So deep in thought was he, he hadn't noticed anyone near the tent until he was standing right in front of the entrance. A movement out of the corner of his eye had him turning his head. "Elena?"

"Peter, I had to see you. I have information about the spy."

All thought of his personal problems vanished. "Tell me."

"I have seen proof that Maxine is the spy. She was talking to someone on a communicator, a new American invention from what I saw."

Peter rubbed the back of his neck a moment before speaking. "America is a very inventive nation, but that doesn't mean she is a spy. Perhaps she was talking to her family."

"No, I, I heard her say, '*yes, sir.*' You don't call family sir, Peter."

Elena was right. What she overheard of Max's conversation was worrisome. "I expect not. Where is this communicator?"

"She keeps it in her pack."

Peter didn't like what he was hearing but he couldn't ignore the information. "Leave now and don't tell anyone until I investigate the truth of your claim."

She pouted. "I wouldn't lie about such a thing."

"I know." He glanced over to Max's tent. She was there, standing still, watching him and Elena. "I just want to be certain before any accusations are made."

A smug smile grew on Elena's lips as she looked at Max. "She's seen me, she knows I have told you. What are you going to do?"

He rubbed his chin as Max ducked back inside the tent. "Nothing tonight. We are all tired. Go and I will speak with you in the morning and tell you my decision."

"Yes, I am tired. Good night, Peter."

Peter watched Elena walk to the tent Max slept in. She had a spring in her step he hadn't seen for quite some time. He shook his head. She was happy she caught Max in a compromising position. But he couldn't believe Max was a spy any more than he could believe Karina was one.

He tried to shake the tension out of his shoulders, but something was wrong, something had his senses buzzing. Sometimes when he perused building plans, he would get the same feeling and would take apart the plans and piece them back together again until he found what was making him concerned. Every time, he would find a missing building process or a missing ingredient in the plans, but what was he not seeing here? He gazed out over the dark camp where only the night guards marched along their lines. It all seemed peaceful and it was hard to think that they would all be fighting for their lives once again soon.

He shook his head. Max was no more a spy than he was—he knew that in his heart and soul.

He went into his tent, hoping sleep would give him clarity.

He climbed into bed and covered the thin blankets with his greatcoat, deciding to find the thing Max had that Elena insisted was a communication device. He decided it must be a family trinket that would only mean something to Max and Max alone. His last thought before sleep overtook him was, why not just ask her about it?

FROM CAFÉS TO COSSACKS

THE NEXT MORNING PETER SAT UP, DETERMINED TO ASK Max about the thing Elena saw, but he frowned. Every other time he'd asked her about something that had him concerned, she'd brushed him off. He wondered if she'd do that this time.

He glanced around the tent to find Yegor and Vanya and their packs, gone.

He slid out of the uncomfortable, lumpy trundle bed and stretched his back into the correct position. It was still dark outside, so it wasn't too late.

Someone clearing their throat had him spinning around to find Vanya stepping over the threshold.

"Peter, we have just spoken to our men from Kasanka. Their intel is that a trap is set on the other side of Vysun River. We must find another route but worse is, they say the spy from Ilya's troop is amongst us. I am sorry, but Yegor and I talked with the soldiers and we believe they are innocent and loyal to Ilya and the Whites. We also believe neither Elena nor you would do such a thing."

Vanya sat down on the only chair in the room and put his face in his hands. "I do not want to think such a thing, but there can be no other conclusion. The spy is Maxine."

Peter listened without interrupting, trying to clear the sleep from his mind and take in what Vanya was saying. Vanya of all people would not suggest Max was a spy if he didn't think it possible. He liked Max. Now if it was Yegor or Elena making the accusations, Peter would be less inclined to believe them, but Vanya? He stared at the man who was clearly troubled to have said such a thing.

Vanya shook his head. "It is hard to believe, is it not?"

"It is, and I don't believe it. But having said that, how could the Reds know our route? Could it have been someone from Ilya's troop? Perhaps someone who didn't accompany

Ilya on his mission, yes, that makes more sense than to suggest Max is a spy."

Vanya stood up. "I do not know, Peter, but we must be wary of everyone and that includes Max."

Peter frowned at that. "Even Karina?"

"*Da*, all of us know she does not want to go to Denmark, she wants to stay in Russia. What better way to do that than stop you from taking her to the sea?"

"Now you are just clutching at straws, my friend. Even as young as Karina is, she would not endanger herself for such a cause."

"*Da*, you are right."

"Where is Max now?"

"Still asleep, I think."

"You and Yegor find us another route and I will join you soon."

"*Da*."

Peter packed his sack while arguing with himself. *Ask her.* No. If she was a spy, would she not lie? He figured if he found a communication device then she would have no choice but to tell the truth. He would have the proof in his hands. *What if it is only a keepsake? She will be angry you didn't just ask her.* Peter threw his sack on his back. If it was a keepsake, he would expect her to understand his actions. They were at war, no one was above suspicion.

He hurried outside into the still dark morning and was surprised to spot Elena and Karina walking away from their tent. He'd have to wait to find out where they were going so early in the morning because right then he had a mission to do.

Stepping lightly, he made his way inside the tent. Something snapped underfoot, and he froze. The sound was loud to his ears, but Max didn't move, and he was glad she slept soundly though he didn't know how she could in the middle of a war. He peeked in the room.

Spying the backpack on the chair, he moved to it and opened it. He dug his hand down to the bottom and felt something hard and round within some cloth. Pulling it out carefully with one hand so as not to break it, he placed the pack back on the chair with his other.

"What the blazes are you doing?"

Peter started and nearly dropped the item; he had to use both hands to hold it steady. Not only was she awake but she was already standing right in front of him, fully dressed.

"You are awake." He knew it was a stupid thing to say, but he couldn't think of anything else at that moment. Her clothes threw him. Had she been awake the whole time?

"You knew someone entered your room?"

"Of course, I did, I'm not an idiot. And I knew it was you without having to see your face."

"So you pretended to be asleep?" He was still trying to sort out his thoughts. What explanation he could give for sneaking into her room and rifling through her things.

Her gaze went to the thing in his hands. "I was up and ready to leave when I heard you skulking outside. You're not very quiet, you know?"

He thought he'd been more than furtive. "You have amazing hearing."

"I wouldn't say that. Now why are you here and why do you have my belongings in your hands?"

"Elena..."

She rolled her eyes to the ceiling at the mention of Elena's name and waved her hand about. "Go on then."

"Elena saw you with what she thought was a communication device. She was worried you were a spy. Vanya and Yegor are also concerned. We have intel that the Reds know our route and have lain a trap. If we didn't find that out, we would have driven right into their hands this very day."

"So you thought you'd come in here and find out if they were right? Why didn't you just ask me?"

Regaining control of his thoughts, Peter unfolded the shirt around the thing and stared at what must have been a keepsake because he'd never seen anything like it before.

He turned the item around in his hands. The leaves were real gold. "I don't believe you're a spy, Max, but I know you are hiding something from me and if I did ask perhaps you wouldn't have answered. Perhaps you would have brushed me off just like you had when I asked about you and Ilya."

"So yes, I could have asked you. But if you were hiding something, would you have told me?"

Her gaze never left her keepsake, and he threw the egg-shaped ornament into the air and caught it again.

Max leapt forward, plucked it from his hands and quickly stepped back out of his reach. He moved to reclaim it.

She glared at him. "Stay where you are."

He stopped still and asked, "What is it?"

Hugging it to her chest, she raised her brows. "Would you believe it's a family heirloom?"

"I might have if you'd shown it to me before, but now? Seeing the way, you protect it? No. Now tell me the truth."

"You can't handle the truth."

She laughed and Peter frowned. "What is so funny?"

"Sorry, I think I just said a line from some movie."

"Movie?"

Still full of mirth, she said, "It doesn't matter, just know, if I told you the truth and nothing but the truth, you wouldn't believe me."

She was talking and acting like a madwoman. How could she be so likable, so kissable, one minute and seemingly deranged the next? Thinking to change the subject away from the keepsake, Peter asked again, "Tell me the truth. How do you know Ilya so well?"

"I don't really, I only met him that night you brought me to his camp."

"Max, please, I'm trying to help you. We have intel that there is a trap on the route only us and Ilya knew we were taking. Somebody must have relayed our plans to the enemy and Elena is convinced you are the spy."

She pierced Peter with a look. "You believe that?" She hugged the egg closer to her chest. "I am not a spy. I told you, you wouldn't believe me if I told you the truth."

"Something is wrong about you; I know I'm right. How is it Ilya wasn't surprised to see you appear that night at the camp? What is it you're not telling me?"

She threw a hand up in the air. "Why don't you ask Ilya?"

"He is too far away, and you know it." Peter's ire rose. She was playing with him. Didn't she realize how serious this was? "If my men hear you talk this way, they will insist you be arrested."

A flicker of fear passed through her eyes, but she shrugged.

He didn't know what else to do to make her tell him the truth, so he pulled his handgun out of its holder and pointed it at her. Maybe that would get her attention. "Now tell me, how do you know him so well?"

Her shoulders shook with laughter. Peter tightened his grip on the gun. What was the matter with her? Why was she acting like a madwoman?

"Are you going to shoot me?" Her bottom lip dropped in a sulk. "I thought you liked me?"

Her false bravado only made him angrier. He gritted his teeth. "Tell me."

She let out a long, loud breath. "Okay, Ilya didn't know

me, but he knew my parents and we hit it off from the moment we met. He's a nice guy."

Peter had seen Ilya deep in battle, had been on the receiving end of his ire, and the man never smiled, never joined in the celebrations of a win. "A nice guy?"

"Yes, he's wonderful and he helped me figure out what I needed in my life. I mean, I mightn't have been the best student, but he never got angry with me. Now you on the other hand, you're angry now, aren't you? And," she looked Peter in the eye, "he knows my secret."

"So you are hiding something. What secret?"

"I never said I wasn't, but as I said before, you won't believe me."

He blew out a puff of air. He wanted her to trust him. He put the gun back in its holster. "Even though you are acting insane right now, I do trust you, Max, and I will believe anything you tell me."

She pressed her lips together and sat on the bed, shaking her head. She gazed at him with her soulful blue eyes and patted the mattress with her hand for Peter to sit down also. He did and she took in a deep breath.

"Okay, here goes." She held the keepsake with one hand on the top. "This here is a time-travelling device. I am from the future."

Peter leaned back and frowned at her. "The truth, Max."

"I told you, you wouldn't believe me. Ilya knows. He knew my parents time travelled and he was their contact in this time."

"Ilya thinks you are from the future?"

"He knows I am from the future."

"You were right, I don't believe it, and if you don't trust me enough to tell me the truth there is no hope for us. I won't arrest you but you will have to leave."

Her eyes clouded with sadness and she dipped her head and gazed at the orb. "Fine, I'll leave," she said quietly.

She turned the top of the keepsake.

Peter thought it must be a bomb but before he could dive to the floor, she grabbed his arm. Her voice floated to his ears as if from a distance away. "But you're coming with me."

Everything went black.

His first thought was that she had blown them both up. But another thought immediately followed the first: how could he think if he was dead? His body seemed pulled in all directions and before he could dwell on the feeling, he crashed into something hard. He must have closed his eyes at the explosion because now as he realized his body was intact and he had stopped moving, he peeked one eye open.

CHAPTER 19

Max held out her hand to Peter. He would be feeling disorientated and would need something to hold on to, something familiar. She smirked thinking how she offered herself for the cause.

"Max?"

"Yes, here, let me help you."

Accepting her hand, he got to his feet and stared at the two other people in the bleak room.

Garrett frowned and Bree grinned, looking at Peter and Max in turns.

"So, you brought him back with you? Why?" Bree glanced at their entwined hands. "Or is that a silly question?"

Peter let go of Max's hands and Max was worried. How was she going to explain what she just did to him? What was she thinking? Of course, she wasn't thinking, she couldn't have been.

"I knew he wouldn't believe me when I told him the truth and he didn't. I didn't know what else to do so I brought him here." She turned to Peter. "I'm sorry. I probably shouldn't have done that."

"No, you shouldn't have," Garrett said. "Take him back now."

"What? No, now that we're here I may as well get it over with." Max took Peter's arm and guided him to a stool. "Sit down and listen. This is my time, your future. And this," she waved her arm around the scant room with its cinder-block walls, "is our basement." She smiled at him. "I know it's not much but it's functional."

Peter's eyes glazed over and Max thought he was going to faint.

"Are you all right? Peter, speak to me."

He rubbed his forehead. "I don't like parlor games."

"It's not a game, I promise. You didn't believe me when I told you the truth, so I figured I would show you." She swept her arm in the air. "See? This is the basement of our house. Oh and that's my little brother, Garrett, and this is our cousin, Briana, but we call her Bree."

"Hi," Bree said. "You don't look so hot."

He frowned at her. "I am not hot."

"Well you sort of are, but I meant, you look sick."

"Where are we, Maxine?" Peter demanded. "Am I imprisoned?"

"I haven't captured you, you ninny, I've brought you to my home."

He narrowed his eyes as he looked around the room. "This looks like a prison."

"I told you, it's a basement. We're underground, that's why there are no windows. See, there are steps. You want to come up into the house?"

"No, I want to go back to Karina. She is in danger."

"I know, but she'll be fine while we're here. Trust me."

As soon as Max said the words, she knew he'd lose it and she was right. His blood heated so quickly; it made his face go red.

Peter rose and loomed over her. "I do not trust you any longer. Take me back now!"

Max stood her ground and folded her arms across her chest. "No. Not until you listen to me. I am not a spy, I only care about getting Karina and you safely out of Russia but if you're going to be mean, I'll keep you here until you're nice."

"Max," Garrett said. "You're scaring him. Back away."

Max laughed at that. "I'm scaring him?"

He was the one standing over her, scowling at her as if he was going to strangle her any moment.

Peter's gaze changed from ire to confusion. "I am not scared but I am confused as to why you would do this to me. Did our kisses mean nothing to you? Was everything a charade?"

"No Peter. No. This isn't a prison, I promise. Surely you have basements in Denmark? Or cellars?"

He looked around the room again, this time taking in the space more keenly. "Basements can be prisons."

"I suppose, but really, this one isn't." She gazed into his eyes, willing him to trust her. "Please believe me."

Peter's hand moved to his waist, just above where Max knew his gun was positioned.

"Tell me why you have brought me here," Peter asked.

Max couldn't answer; the only thing she thought to do was leap at Peter and kick him in the jaw, not too hard, but just hard enough for him to fall back off balance. Her hands dived into his coat, pulled out the handgun, and stepping back, she pointed the barrel at him.

Confusion washed over Peter's face. "What are you doing?"

"If you move, I'll shoot you," Max said.

Bree gasped and covered her mouth. "You wouldn't?"

Garrett stepped forward and plucked the gun out of her hand. "No, she wouldn't."

"Garrett," Max whined. "Peter didn't know that."

Peter rubbed his chin, slowly looking from Max to Garrett and back again. "I do believe he is your brother."

"You do?" Max asked, her eyes widening and a hopeful smile on her face.

"Only a brother would know you so well."

"If there's no more fighting, I'll make some coffee," Bree said. "Or would you prefer tea, Peter?"

"Coffee would be most welcome."

Max followed Bree to the stairs but they both turned at Garrett's voice.

"Not you, you stay here until they're upstairs." He pointed the gun at Peter.

Peter tipped his head forward in a slight bow. "Of course."

Bree took Max's hand and they climbed the stairs. "Was that so he couldn't grab one of us?"

"Yep, not bad thinking. Peter would have probably done something stupid like that. He is scared a bit, I guess."

"I would be. Actually, when I travelled with your parents, I was terrified."

"You travelled often with them?"

"Just the once."

Max caught sadness in Bree's eyes as she turned and headed for the kitchen, but with Peter foremost in her mind, she tucked the observation away to ask about later.

Garrett ducked through the door and raised his brows at Max. "He's all yours."

Peter stepped into the hallway as Garrett left and scanned the room. His eyes flickered at the décor but his face showed no expression whatsoever.

Max waved her hand about. "This is my home."

Peter walked into the entry, gazing around and up the stairs then back at Max. "It looks like a normal home, but so is the home the Romanovs are imprisoned in. It appears the Bolsheviks prefer homes to formal prisons."

"Really? Does this look like any Russian home to you?" But she frowned as she took in her home through Peter's eyes. The walls could have been from the early nineteenth century with the tiny blue vintage floral wallpaper, and of all things to have on display on the small table next to the stairs, there was a Russian stacked doll. She bit the inside of her cheek and watched Peter take in the paintings on the walls.

"Good, aren't they? My brother painted them all."

He gave a quick nod and strolled to the front sitting room door. Max grimaced. Even the furniture looked like it came from his time, maybe not Russia, but England, and he'd recognize the style. She tried to think of something so modern, it would have him question his assumptions, but what?

Of course, the television. She scooted past him into the sitting room and pointed to the TV. "There, you've never seen anything like that, have you?"

"A black square?"

She scooped up the controller and pressed on. "Not just a black square."

The screen sprang into life and Peter jumped back. "What is this?"

She flicked through the stations. "I told you, it's a television, it shows moving pictures, movies, advertisements, all sorts of shows."

"It's magic."

"No, everyone's house has at least one, some have one in every room, even the bathroom."

Peter stepped closer to the TV and peered at an ad for peanut butter. The kids in the ad were eating it from the jar with teaspoons, licking and sticking the gooey spoons on their tongues.

"That is an ad for peanut butter, everyone loves peanut butter and the people making the ads hope that people will buy their brands."

"I understand the concept of advertising, I don't understand the square full of people."

"They're not really in the TV, they have been filmed and then shown on the TV." She flicked the channel again. An old episode of *The Golden Girls* was showing. "They make shows like plays, or like you see at picture theaters, that people can watch in their own homes. This one is old, but you can see they are different. Look at their clothes—not exactly Russian wear, are they?"

He gazed at Max and back at the TV. He pulled his hands down his face and neck. "I don't know how you've done it, and I am not fooled, but I am in admiration of your people's talents."

"Max," Bree called. "Coffee's ready."

Max smashed her lips together and looked at Peter. "Come on, maybe some real coffee will make you believe me."

※

ONCE THEY WERE SEATED AT THE DINING TABLE AND BREE and Max poured the hot espresso for everyone, they all relapsed into silence.

Max enjoyed the aroma and taste of the drink while keeping an eye on Peter. She figured she had better give him time to come to terms with his predicament.

Peter behaved while drinking his coffee, although his eyes never stopped moving. Max guessed there was a lot to take in. When she first time travelled, she knew she was going back in time so wasn't surprised to find everything and everyone different, but poor Peter had no such prior knowledge. She tried to smile when his gaze met hers, but he immediately tightened his jaw and went back to scanning his surroundings.

Max finally said, "What do you think?"

He slowly placed his cup on the table. "I don't know what to think. Either you are a spy and your people have engineered what they think the future would look like, or I am indeed in the future. Neither thought sits well with me."

"I'm sorry."

"You may as well know," Bree said. "This is your future but it's our present. The paintings are real, and Garrett here painted most of them. Those there," she pointed to a collage of photographs, "are pictures taken by Max and Garrett's parents." She stood up and moved closer. "See that one? That's Max when she was about ten."

He got up and peered closer at the picture, at Max, then back at the picture. "I can see a slight resemblance. These are photographs?" He touched them. "They are of the finest quality."

"Yeah, we have way better tech than the early twentieth century."

"Tech?"

"Technology," Garrett said. "But I prefer brushes and paint to cameras."

Peter moved around the room studying the paintings. "You are extremely talented."

"Thanks. How about more coffee, Bree? I'll help you."

Bree hesitated, apparently not wanting to miss anything, but finally nodded and left the room with Garrett.

Left alone, Max wished she'd got Peter's gun back before Garrett left. Peter's displeasure in her was tangible. "You're quiet," she said.

"I need time to sort through my own thoughts."

"Okay, I can understand that. Why don't I go and help with the coffee? Give you time alone."

He raised his brows. "Yes, that would be acceptable."

"Great, I'll be back soon." She left the dining room but closed the two sliding white doors. Maybe if he had time to think, he'd come around. She let go of the doors and scoffed. Perhaps not a good idea to let him roam around by himself. She clicked the lock and stood back, looking at the glossy white-painted wood.

A thump on the doors sounded from the other side. Max grimaced. He wouldn't be happy about being locked in.

※

Peter withdrew his hand from the door. He should have realized Max would lock him in, but he thought she'd be so happy he was cooperating that she would just leave him there.

He turned around and surveyed the room. The dining room wasn't much different to his own at home. Smaller than in his chalet, but still large enough to tell him they weren't poor people. The long wooden table was old and the white paint so thin, the wood grains showed through. Perhaps they were thin on money after all. Three chairs sat on either side but the table could seat eight if an extra two chairs at the ends were added, where his highly polished wooden table sat twelve comfortably.

He quickly hurried to the window in the center of the end wall and pulled back the pretty yellow curtains. The vista outside was beautiful: rolling green grassy field, a mountain range in the distance and trees that must have been centuries old, they were so large. He tried to open the window, but it too was locked. He stood looking out over the grounds. Had Max planned to imprison him there? Her locking the door didn't prove that to him, but why else would the windows be locked?

He pressed his forehead to the cool glass and looked down. Pretty yellow flowerbeds wound around the house. He kinked his neck to look along the outside of his prison. The bricks, also coated with thin white paint, were small rectangles and as far as he could tell it was an ordinary country house.

He turned away from the window and sighed. What was this place? He walked around examining the pictures on the walls, noting the pale lemon wallpaper, embossed with flowers. Some of the picture frames were also thinly painted wood, some white, some blue, and some yellow. The paintings, landscapes and horses, and portraits were indeed done skillfully. Garrett, if that was his real name and if he really did the work, was exceptionally talented.

Peter peered at a painting. A group of two older and five younger people. He guessed the older couple was the parents and the younger ones, their children. A dark red-haired woman and a blonde woman stood to one side of the couple and waited, while a dark-haired woman's blue eyes stared at him from between a fiery red-haired woman who looked like Briana, and a young man who could only be Garrett. He trailed his hand down the thick oil paint that was Max's face. "Max," he whispered.

She was younger, maybe at least ten years younger, a teenager really, but it was Max. Could she have told the truth?

He crossed to the opposite wall. More exquisite photographs of the children, and he searched out Max in every one. They were all lovely girls and women—even Garrett and the man Peter thought to be their father were quite handsome, he supposed—but Max stood out as the fairest. She was the most beautiful.

Peter shook his head and surveyed the room once more. Could he have traveled in time? Could he be in the future?

The sound of the door unlocking brought Peter out of his ruminations.

Max walked in with a tray. Coffee and... He peered at the plate. Apricot sweet pastries. How did she know they were his favorite?

He gazed into her worried eyes, transfixed for a moment.

She placed the tray on the table and looked at him, her face full of questions, but all he could do was stare at her. She was from the future? How could this be?

She sucked in her lips then let out a puff of air. "This was a mistake. I'll take you back."

Peter started. "No."

"No?"

"No." He rubbed his chin and pierced her with his gaze. "Now that I'm here I'd like to learn more of your life."

"You believe me?"

"I am beginning to. Yes."

Max's shoulders relaxed and she smiled. "Good, because I didn't want to hurt you."

He grinned. "You wouldn't have." He put out his arm and bent his head in a bow. "A tour, my lady?"

She placed her hand on his forearm like she'd seen Izzy do with Edward. "Sure."

※

Once she'd shown him the house, Max led him out onto the back patio. He stopped at the railing and looked at the panorama before him. Max followed his eyes to the perfectly mowed lawn, the precisely edged garden beds, the fruit and nut grove, the rolling hills, and his gaze finally rested on her.

"You have a team of gardeners?"

"One. He comes up from town once a week or so. I think he brings his son sometimes. He's good, huh?"

"We have a team of gardeners and they cannot do what your man does in such a short time. How does he do it?"

"He has machines to help him, like lawn mowers he sits on and edge trimmers, electric garden shears..." Max could see she was losing him. "Just modern machinery will have to do."

"I would like to see some of this machinery."

Uh-oh. Peter was an intelligent man and if he saw something he understood, he might go back and change history by inventing it himself or having someone else do it. She couldn't risk that. In fact, she had to keep him away from anything that might be replicable. "Maybe another time."

Back inside, Max hesitated. Where could she take him that didn't have stuff he could learn from? She checked the wall clock. Lunchtime, so she guided him back to the dining room. At least there, there was nothing he could examine too closely.

Peter paused on the threshold. "I would like to spend some time in the library."

"Oh, no, you don't. You're not going to read any modern stuff. I don't even know if we have books from your time there."

"That's what I want to see, modern writings."

"No, maybe another time but not this one. It's all too much for you to take in. I shouldn't have even shown you the TV."

"I am quite relaxed and open to all you have to show me. I am not intimidated by you, your relatives or your house. I would like to investigate more. Perhaps you could take me into town?"

"Have some lunch and I'll think about it."

Bree had already placed small bottles of cold sodas and

more coffee on the table. Garrett brought in a platter of toasted ham, cheese and tomato sandwiches.

Peter's eyes widened at the display. He picked up a bottle of cola. "What is this?"

"A drink," Max said. "Try it."

He carefully took a sip. Pleasure washed over his face and he tipped the bottle up and drank a long gulp. "I like it."

Garrett laughed. "I knew you would." He pointed to the platter. "Try those."

Peter looked around the table and frowned.

Max guessed he was trying to find some cutlery, so she picked up a triangle. "Use your hands."

"Saves on washing up," Bree said. "And I hate washing up."

"You hate cooking more," Garrett said.

"True."

They made small talk while they ate. Garrett seemed to warm to Peter the more he spoke to him. He wanted to know everything about his work, especially building bridges.

Peter was more than forthcoming with what he knew. He also seemed to like the sandwiches because he ate nearly all of them.

"We'd better go back," Max said.

"Once Karina is out of danger then I would like to return and stay longer."

Garrett stood up. "Probably not a good idea, pal. You have to go back."

"But why? You have stayed for longer in my time."

"Yeah, but that's different."

"How?"

Max patted his arm and stood up. "It just is. Come on, we have to get Karina to that ship."

CHAPTER 20

P eter found himself in the tent sitting on the bed beside Max. He was astonished—her cousin had sent them back to the precise time they left.

Max wrapped up her time travel device, tucked it back into her bag, and grinned at Peter.

His jaw tightened. "That was interesting." He struggled with the reality of it all. Had they really gone to the future, or had she somehow medicated him to think he had? "Did we really go to your time? In America? In the future?"

"Yes, but it's probably best not to tell anyone. They might think you're mad and lock you away."

"I don't intend on telling anyone." A memory of Elena and Karina leaving the camp early that morning came to his mind. "Stay here, I have something I need to attend to."

"Sure, but aren't we supposed to leave early this morning?"

"Yes, but first I have to speak to Vanya. Stay here."

Peter's heart picked up speed with every thought. If Max wasn't the spy, who then? Not Vanya or Yegor, and Vanya was adamant that Ilya's soldiers were loyal. Elena? He rushed out of the tent and sprinted in the direction Elena and Karina took earlier.

His gait slowed as he neared a group of trees. What if they were doing female things? He remembered there was a small stream close to the camp. If they were bathing, he couldn't very well go crashing in on them. He stopped and listened; a bird tweeted in the distance and another answered. He frowned. They didn't sound like any birds he'd heard before though he had to admit, he didn't know every bird in Russia and especially what birds were found in Mykolaiv.

A trill of tweets sounded closer to Peter. He turned in the direction away from the stream and held his breath. Footfalls. More than two and heavy. So not Elena and Karina then. He crept forward, bending low and scanning underfoot for any branches or twigs that might give him away.

Male voices speaking in Russian floated to his ears. A scream. Karina. Peter pulled out his gun and swept forward, going from tree to tree, and soon stopped dead still.

Three Bolshevik soldiers were aiming rifles at Elena and Karina.

"Why are you doing this?" Karina cried out. "I thought you were my friend."

"I was never your friend."

Elena? Her lip rose in a sneer and her glare positively poured pure hatred. Peter couldn't believe he could have missed her true nature for so long.

Elena ordered the soldiers about. "Mikal, take her and you two go ahead and clear our path."

Two of the soldiers ran in the direction of the hills as the last one grabbed Karina and she cried out in pain. Peter hurtled through the melting snow and hit the soldier's head hard with the butt of his gun. The man grunted and fell at his feet as Peter, aiming his gun at Elena, kicked the soldier's weapon away.

"Get it, Karina."

She was sobbing and her eyes were wild with fright, but she did as she was told.

"You," Peter said to Elena as he waved his gun in the camp's direction. "Back to camp."

Something slammed into his back and he fell forward, air bursting from his lungs.

Twisting his head around to better see his assailant, he couldn't believe his eyes. "Kolya?"

The man was Ilya's trusted lieutenant, but Peter couldn't take time questioning the soldier; he pulled his knees up and pushed the big man off with his feet. Scrambling up, he tried to hold his gun up but Kolya was too quick. He kicked it out of Peter's hand. And aimed his rifle at Peter's head.

"Peter," Karina called.

Peter glanced her way. Elena was circling behind her.

"Karina! Run. Run now."

At the snapping of Elena's foot on a twig, Karina turned and shot. She missed Elena but was running toward the camp without looking behind.

Peter glared at Kolya. "Why are you wearing a Bolshevik uniform?"

"I am Bolshevik. The Whites are overrun and have already lost the revolution. Is not that so, Sister?"

"It is, Brother," Elena said. "There is no place for royals in our new Russia."

Kolya laughed and clicked the trigger back.

"No," Elena said. "Do not kill him."

"Why not? He is the enemy of Russia."

"Our mission is to kill the princess, not him." She strolled around Peter until she stopped in front of him.

It crossed Peter's mind to attack her, but she was more than an arm's length away and Kolya would shoot him before he could get his hands around her throat.

"You will suffer, Peter. You will regret rejecting me. I will kill Karina and the American infiltrator, but you will live, live to regret your decisions for the rest of your life."

A plane's engine roared into life toward the hills.

The sound of boots running toward them stopped Elena's postulating. "Kolya, go." Elena glared at Peter. "The princess will die, if not by my hand then by others."

She and Kolya ran in the opposite direction.

The soldiers crashed out of the trees and Peter pointed. "That way."

But before the soldiers were even out of sight, the sound of a plane roaring into the morning sky had Peter looking up. A DH4 biplane flew low and he was sure he could see Elena's laughing visage in the back seat.

Max was at Peter's side as the plane disappeared into thickening clouds.

"Are you all right?" Max gazed up into the sky. "Was that a plane? Karina said Elena tried to kidnap her. She didn't know if you'd been killed or not." She turned her gaze on Peter. "How the blazes did they get a plane here without anyone hearing or seeing it?"

"It was probably already here before we arrived. Elena knew our route. We must leave. Now."

With that, he strode back to the camp, Max half trotting, half walking behind him.

Vanya and Yegor caught up. "What happened?"

"We don't have time for me to keep repeating myself. Tell the men to meet me in the mess."

"Wouldn't it be safer to stay with the army?" Max wanted to know.

"No."

Peter increased his gait. He knew he was rude to Max but now that he was back in his own time, back in the midst of the war, there could be no future for them. She had to return to her time and, with Elena wanting her dead, the sooner the better.

Stepping in the mess tent, Peter was glad the commander was there. The man rubbed his bald head behind his ear and his long, curled mustache twitched as Peter neared his table.

He waved a hand for Peter to sit down but Peter shook his head. "My people will be here shortly."

Vanya, Yegor, Ilya's soldiers, and Max hurried into the tent and surrounded the table.

Vanya plucked up some cured meat and began chewing.

The commander glanced at him but said to Peter, "I was surprised to learn Elena was our spy." He swore in Russian. "And Kolya? Ilya will be most disappointed. But now that she has gone, we can accompany you to Odessa."

"*Nyet*. Together we are too many. In fact I would like to leave Dima, Pasha and Feliks. Only Vanya and Yegor will come with Karina and me."

"What?" Max said. "No. I'm coming too."

Peter lowered his voice and grated, "We will discuss this outside." And to Commander Yudenich, he said, "Elena knows the country and she knows all the routes to Odessa. With only one vehicle, perhaps we can find a way not on any map."

"*Da*, perhaps it is for the best." He stood up and shook Peter's hand. "Travel safe, my friend."

Peter bowed and left. Max was close on his heels and she grabbed his arm, pulling him up the moment they were outside.

"What do you think you're doing? You know I can help. Why would you leave me here?"

"I'm not leaving you here, I expect you to go home. Leave Russia and this time. Go back."

"No. *Nyet*. I'm coming with you, at least as far as the port.

Once I know you and Karina are safely on your way, I'll leave."

Her eyes were wide and pleading; fear brewed in them and he knew then she was scared for him. All Peter wanted at that moment was to take her into his arms and tell her everything would be all right, but he had a mission to complete and he would complete it. Karina must be the object of his thoughts and actions. Only her safety mattered. Not him. Not Max.

Karina ran up to them and threw her arms around Peter's neck, her legs swaying in the air. "You are safe. I don't know what I would do without you, my cousin."

He chuckled and after a quick hug untangled her arms and lowered her to the ground. "We leave in the morning."

"I thought we would leave now, so I packed quickly." She turned to Max. "I was going to pack your belongings, Maxine, but I wasn't sure what you would want to take with you. I hope you don't mind."

"No. That's okay. Thanks."

"Max isn't coming."

"Why?" Karina cried. "I want her with me. I need another female with me."

"Why?" Peter asked, frowning in confusion.

Karina lifted her chin in defiance. "Some things are not suitable to discuss in the presence of gentlemen."

Max giggled and Peter knew he was outnumbered. "All right, she can come but only as far as Sevastopol."

Karina took Max's arm and rushed her to their tent.

CHAPTER 21

Max let Karina practically drag her all the way into the tent. Once inside, she faced Max with an expression so bereft, it pained Max's heart.

"I am so sorry, Maxine. I believed Elena's lies. She said you were the spy, the traitor, and I believed her because she was Russian and you were not. Please forgive me."

"There's nothing to forgive, sweetie. I probably would have done the same in your position."

"*Nyet.* You wouldn't have, of that I am sure. Peter trusted you and if he did that should have been enough for me. But Elena had been so kind to me, I don't know how she could have been so cold. Did you know she hated me? She hates all royals."

"I sort of got that feeling, but I hope you learned something from it all. You can't trust everyone you meet, you have to work out if they're lying or not."

"I think I will be better prepared next time. I will not be tricked like that again."

"Never mind, she's gone now and the only thing standing in your way of going home is what? Fifty odd miles?"

"*Da.*" She pulled something out from her pack. "What is this?"

Max stared at it. It was the orb. "What are you doing with that? Hasn't anyone told you people it's bad manners to search in other people's belongings?"

"I wasn't snooping, it fell when I picked up your bag. You never closed it properly." She turned the orb around in her hands. "What is it? I have never seen anything like it before, but it is beautiful."

"It's ah, it's a family heirloom." It wasn't a lie and if Karina had learned anything, she should have been able to tell if Max was lying.

The girl squinted at her as if she was trying to read her mind. "You are telling the truth."

"*Da*, I am. Well done."

Karina beamed. "I should have listened to my instinct. I knew you were a true friend, to me and to Peter, but I just ignored everything my grandmamma had taught me. She would have seen through Elena in a heartbeat."

"She sounds like my kind of woman."

"She is wonderful." Her face fell in sadness. "I hope I will see her again."

Max smiled. "You will. When the Bolsheviks set her free Peter will come and get her and bring her back to you."

"Do you think she will be freed? When?"

"*Da*. I don't think the Bolsheviks mean to kill everyone—they will hold them then let them go, but I'm not sure when that will be. This war could go on for years."

Although the Romanovs were killed in June 1918, Max was pretty sure they did let the lower royals go.

Karina gave her a hug. "Thank you, Maxine. I now have hope in my heart for Grandmamma."

"You are very welcome. Come on or Peter will start shouting at us."

Karina giggled as they hurried out of the tent and ran to the armored car Peter intended to use.

Max handed Yegor her pack and Vanya took Karina's. Max strolled around the vehicle while Vanya and Yegor packed their bags in, but it didn't look the same as the one they drove there. "Is this the same car we used to get here?" Max asked.

"*Da*," Vanya said.

"But it's different."

"*Da*," Yegor said, smiling smugly. "I have added more armor to the front. See?" He stroked his handiwork. "Now we can go anywhere."

Max eyed the new armor and had to admit the skinny Yegor did a good job. The thickness of the metal would have been heavy to move into place. It couldn't have been easy.

"And I have completely waterproofed the cabin, and see this?" Vanya held on to what Max presumed was a handmade snorkel. "I have added a breather pipe, so we may cross deep streams and the motor can breathe."

Max admired the additions. They were crude, but these men had invented the first bull bars and snorkels that future vehicles would utilize every day, not just in war. "That is so neat."

Once they were on their way, Max couldn't help but feel miffed at Peter. He had taken the driver's seat and Vanya the gun, but Peter hadn't spoken to her for the last four hours.

Oh, she still enjoyed gazing at the passing scenery, but without Vanya there to chat to, she was getting more bored by the minute.

They had travelled alongside marshy fields, through small hamlets and wound their way through pretty gorges and forests of big trees. Max recognized the large oaks, chestnuts, pines, and much to her surprise, maples. She looked every which way as they forged their way through the beautiful trees. The scenery was magnificent, and she again made a promise to revisit the Ukraine when she returned to her time period. Karina slept most of the way and while Max tried, her thoughts wouldn't shut up long enough for her to relax and fall asleep.

Finally, heading toward a crop of closely growing trees and underbrush, Max asked, "Can we get through there?"

He answered in one word. *"Da."*

And at first Yegor's addition easily pushed the brush down and they drove over it without a worry, but the bushes got thicker, their main trunks hardier and their branches stronger. The car stopped with a jerk and Max let out a gasp.

She grinned at Peter. "Oops. I think we're stuck."

Peter almost growled at her and pushed his door open, but it wouldn't open very far so he had to squeeze through the narrow opening out of the car.

Vanya crawled out of the gun hatch and Yegor followed him. They stood staring at the shrubbery net that had caught their vehicle.

Max turned to Karina to tell her to stay there, but the girl was pale and staring wide-eyed out of the right-hand window. "What is it?"

Karina didn't answer so Max looked in the same direction and on top of a rise some distance from them, soldiers scurried along the apex. "Blast. Stay here."

Max scrambled out her side, her door having opened without obstruction, and high-kneed it over the fallen brush to the men. She pulled Peter and Vanya to the ground. "Duck." She then threw her voice as far as Yegor. "Yegor, get down."

Thankfully, they were well trained to take orders, and all did as they were told.

Peter tried to stand back up. "No, look." Max pointed over the shrubbery to the rise.

"Have they seen us?" Peter asked.

"I don't think so. We're pretty crammed in here."

"Perhaps the brush is protecting us," Yegor said.

Max smiled. "Perhaps."

"Vanya, get back to the gun," Peter said. "Yegor come with me."

They began to scramble through the growth and Max followed. Peter turned back. "Stay here and protect Karina."

Max narrowed her eyes at him but nodded and stopped. They continued sneaking in a semicircle to the rise and she waited. She decided to let them go ahead a bit then began her own journey circling around in the opposite direction to the rise. She figured she could come up behind the Reds if Peter and Vanya were spotted and if they weren't, she would just stay out of sight and sneak back to the car before anyone knew she was missing.

Keeping her eyes on the rise, she crept through and over the vegetation like a panther on the prowl. A snap of a branch breaking had her stopping abruptly. She screwed up her face at the sound of another crack. It had to be Peter; he was too heavy footed to be creeping up on the enemy. If she was with him, she'd make him stay still and go ahead herself. Why didn't Vanya do just that?

Peter might have been in charge of protecting Karina, but he wasn't a soldier. He had no formal training, just what he'd learned fighting with Ilya. Vanya should oversee covert missions.

Breathing a sigh of relief at the cessation of snapping twigs and heavy-booted falls, Max continued up through the brush. It didn't take her long to get to the fringe of the bush where she hunkered down and took stock of her surroundings. The shrubbery ceased just before the apex of the rise and while she saw a soldier now and then, she was becoming increasingly certain it was the same one.

He walked a few steps down the rise and another soldier joined him. They spoke in Russian, but Max thought she recognized a word—dead or death, she wasn't sure, but the conversation was clearly upsetting. They patted one another's shoulders and went back up and out of sight.

Max spotted Vanya crawling out of the brush and up the rise on his stomach alone. Maybe he did stop Peter from crashing into the enemy camp after all.

He peeked over then waved his hand for Peter to join him. He did and they stayed there for some moments before a shout sounded. They ducked but no shots were fired. Max frowned. In the war games she'd taken part in in her training, if she or any of her troop spotted the enemy sneaking up on them, they would have shot. She scrambled higher and stared at six soldiers standing in front of two medics pointing rifles in Vanya and Peter's direction.

On a hunch, Max stood up and called out, "They have no ammo."

Peter couldn't believe he heard Max's voice. Had he or had he not told her to stay with Karina? What if this was a trap? What if more soldiers were right at that moment attacking the car and Yegor? He glared at her but assessed what she said was true and stood up. The soldiers didn't fire their weapons. He stormed over to her. "What are you doing here? This could be a trap. Karina is in danger."

"She's fine. Look at them—without any ammo, they're sitting ducks and they know it."

Peter studied the soldiers once more. They were still aiming their rifles. "If they don't have bullets, why are they still holding their rifles?"

"They're hoping to bluff us, and it looks like they have done just that to Vanya."

Peter glanced over; Vanya was holding his weapon high in the air as if surrendering.

"Put your gun down, Vanya," Max shouted. "They're not going to shoot you."

Vanya turned a confused face in their direction and shouted to the soldiers in Russian.

"He asked if they had ammunition," Peter said.

"Da," one of the soldiers called back. Then he yelled something else in Russian.

Vanya looked at Peter and the soldiers in turn, not seeming to know what to do.

Max shot into the dirt in front of the soldiers. They didn't shoot and glancing at one another, threw down their weapons.

"Get something to tie them up with," Peter said to Yegor.

※

ONCE THEY HAD THEM TIED AND QUIET, PETER SPOKE IN Russian.

"I told them we'd radio for help and our troops should be here by sunset. All they had to do was stay there and even though they are now prisoners of war, they would be well looked after."

Max looked around their makeshift camp. "Tell them we're going to borrow some stuff. Vanya, grab that coil of rope, and Yegor, can you get me two strong poles?"

Vanya hesitated and looked at Peter.

Peter didn't know what she had in mind but nodded to Vanya. "Go."

Leaving Max with Vanya and Yegor to do her bidding, Peter climbed into the vehicle and radioed the camp they'd left that morning. Once he'd given the coordinates he scuttled into the back seat to Karina. "Are you well?"

"*Da*, but I still can't believe Elena would have killed me."

"Me either, but how can we know other's true minds? They are hidden from us and while we can try to trust people, we have to always remain wary that they could disappoint us."

Karina eyed Peter with raised brows. "Are you talking about Elena or Maxine?"

Peter gazed out of the window at Max hauling on the coil of rope.

"Ah, Maxine," Karina said. "How has she disappointed you? Is she not trustworthy?"

"She is trustworthy, I have no doubt about that."

"You are in love with her and she has rejected you then?"

"I don't think this is a conversation I should be having with a sixteen-year-old girl."

Her back straightened. "I am seventeen, Peteor."

"You never told anyone you had a birthday."

"I told Elena and she said she would get the cook to make a cake at camp but," she gazed at her hands in her lap, "that was before she was revealed as a traitor. I guess she was never going to do it. Another lie."

He took her hands in his. "I am sorry, Karina. I am sorry for missing your birthday and I am sorry I've dragged you across Russia and I am sorry for your grandmother's loss."

She squeezed his hands and smiled. "You will hold a ball for me when we return to Denmark."

He laughed. "I will, will I?"

"*Da,* and while I have not enjoyed travelling with you and watching my Russia torn asunder by war, I understood the reason and I do thank you for saving me from the Bolsheviks and for protecting me since that day. When she comes to peace, perhaps I can return one day."

From the little Max had told him, it would soon be a very different Russia. "Perhaps."

She squeezed his hands again. "But Peter, I have not lost my grandmother. When the war is over, I hope you will return and bring her back to me, to Denmark."

Peter brought her small hands to his mouth and kissed them. "It is good you keep your hope for her safety, but I do not know if that will be possible, Karina."

"Maxine said it is possible and she told me not to give up hope."

"Maxine told you this?"

"Da."

As Karina placed her hands back in her lap, Peter studied Max. She wouldn't have told Karina that if it weren't true. Perhaps the Bolsheviks weren't cold-blooded murders after all. Perhaps they had compassionate hearts and would set the old woman and her companions free.

"I hope you are right."

"I am."

The car lurched and Karina let out a small cry as Max ducked her head in the driver's window. "You two okay?"

Peter nodded.

"You wanna drive? We're pulling the car out now."

Max retreated back out the window as Peter climbed into the driver's seat.

"Stick it in reverse and I'll let you know when to drive back."

Peter placed his hands on the steering wheel and half turned so he could see over his shoulder and through the slits of armor covering the rear window.

Karina was perched on her knees, peering through the slits.

"She does talk strangely, doesn't she?"

He chuckled. *"Da."*

Max hurried to join Vanya and Yegor. They had tied the rope to the back of the car and the end to a strong trunked tree. Along the line of unwound rope, they had two log poles looped together at right angles. Vanya picked up one pole and pushed it against the other side of the rope. The car lurched back gently but didn't really move any distance. Yegor did the same with his pole, and again the car lurched but didn't go anywhere. They took turns moving the poles around the rope until finally, the car inched away from the boggy shrub.

Peter kept the car straight while it slowly drifted backwards.

"Now!" Max shouted.

Peter drove the car in reverse for a few meters, stopped the car and hoped out. Admiring Max's handiwork, he smiled at her beaming face. "A winch."

"Yep, and it worked like a beauty. Ready to go?"

Once they were back in their places and winding around the brush to the narrow road used by horses and wagons, Peter searched for any sign of trouble from his position as gunner. Again, his thoughts turned to Max and how she loved the excitement of battle.

The thought of asking her to stay with him had worked its way forward as he spoke with Karina earlier, but again, his logical mind dispelled the notion. She would never be happy in a domestic setting. Even if he included her in the business of the company, she would soon grow bored and hunger for excitement. No. He would set her free to pursue her life's ambitions in her time. There she would be safe and happy, and her happiness was his only concern.

CHAPTER 22

Peter had been quiet since he and Max returned from the future. She could understand him taking time to come to terms with her revelations, but something told her that wasn't it. Something else happened when he saved Karina from Elena and her henchmen. But what? What could Elena have said to make Peter so cold to her?

They were close to the sea when they stopped at another inn for the night. This one was much the same as the last, but bigger and had three stories, the ground floor consisting of the dining room, two or three smaller firelit rooms and the kitchen, and two stories of rooms sharing a bathroom on each floor.

It was still light out, and Max needed fresh air so she went outside for a walk. She entered a dark wooded area. All she could think about was being forced to part with Peter forever. Could she live through that kind of pain? Oh, she could take a bullet and fight hand-to-hand combat if she had to, but going back to her previous life? Without Peter?

She snorted—loudly. She quickly looked around and was thankful no one else was in the wood at that time. She decided she could live without him. After all she had done it before, hadn't she?

Before she met the man, she'd had her life planned as best she could. She would go back to school and spend her days learning how to look after animals, especially horses.

She breathed in the sweet pine smell permeating the air as she trod on the needles. Russia was a beautiful country and she still meant to visit there as soon as possible after she returned to her time.

More crushing pine needles sounded behind her and she turned, arms up, ready to fight.

"Peter." She replaced the gun in its holder. "You should have said something. I could have knocked you out."

"We have to talk."

"Okay, what do you want to talk about?"

"We are nearly at the port and I think it's time we said goodbye. You must return to your time."

"I'm not sure when I'll return. Why are you so eager to see me go?"

He frowned. "I am not eager, but it's best if we didn't spend any more time together. Karina will be safe in two days. The Reds haven't infiltrated this far south, and we must hurry if we are to catch the ship to Romania. It leaves at precisely seven in the morning. If we miss that ship, there won't be another for two weeks."

"I still don't see how my leaving will get you there any quicker."

"Even though I said we were on a safe route, I need to keep my wits about me. Elena is out there somewhere, and I think if you weren't part of our group, she would keep away."

An ache spread over Max's chest. "So, it's about Elena then, not me. She's hell-bent on making you pay for rejecting her whether I'm there or not. Though I can see how she might be more irrational if she sees me. She did find us in one another's arms, even though she doesn't know you're not that interested in me." Max didn't want to leave yet, but Peter was right. Elena was out there, and she would be watching. Although Max understood Elena's hatred for any royals were what made her choose the Bolshevik's side, she was pretty sure, the woman's jealousy of her was what spurred her on in her hunt for Peter. Maybe Elena wouldn't go after the Rosenborgs if Max was out of the picture.

She bent and picked up a pine needle. "Okay. I'll go."

Peter didn't look happy about her agreeing with him in the least. "Now what's wrong?"

He rubbed his face. "I suppose I didn't think you would agree so readily."

"You wanted me to fight with you about it?" She threw the needle down and wiped her hands together. "No point. You're right, it's best if I leave. Karina will be safest without me in the picture."

Peter stepped close and Max went to back away, but he wrapped his arms around her waist and brought her in close. "I am right but Max, I will miss you."

"I'll miss you too," Max whispered, trying not to crawl into his greatcoat with him.

He lifted her chin with his finger. She stared, captured by the hunger in his eyes.

He growled. "If we met in another place, another time, I would not let you go."

"And I wouldn't let you let me go."

His lips crushed against her mouth and she pushed back, accepting his kiss.

They stayed there, exploring and memorizing one another's kiss, touch, smell for who knew how long before Karina's voice broke their rapture.

"Peter? Where are you?"

Peter stepped away from Max and gazed into her eyes. He licked his lips. "I will never forget you."

"And I won't forget you." Max wiped her mouth and turned back to the inn. "Have a nice life, Peter. I'll be gone by morning."

She hurried away before the tears burning her eyes erupted from her soul. Karina came into view and Max turned her head away. "He's back there," she said and quickly went on her way. She refused to cry, and it took an eternity to get to the inn and race to her room. She hadn't realized how far she had walked and now wished she had stayed at the inn. The lump in her throat grew with every step.

Finally, she crashed into her room and slammed the door behind her, fell back against it and slid to the floor. Unable to hold the tears back any longer, she let them flow but had to stop herself from wailing like a banshee. Her low moans croaked around the lump in her throat.

Once the torrent of tears subsided, she hiccoughed and sniffled and wiped her face with the hem of her shirt but the pain stayed with her. Unable to cry any more, she settled on the floor, lying on her side and staring unseeing into the darkness under the bed. Her chest ached, her throat burnt, and her soul, damaged beyond repair, cried dry tears.

She must have fallen asleep sometime during the night because the warmth of the sun on her face had her squinting at the light pouring in through the unshaded window. Memories of the night before came flooding back and new tears began to flow. But she wouldn't give in to them again; it was too unbearable to open herself up like she had. Too painful.

She stretched and groaned. Her whole body ached as if she'd been run over by a tank.

Her eyes spotted her pack under the bed and she stretched out her arm and pulled it toward her, using it as a pillow. Soft at first, she relaxed into it but after a few moments, the hardness of what she knew was the orb bothered her head.

She sat up with a great sigh. *Fine. You want me to go, I'll go.*

She pulled out the orb, unwrapped it and put her hand on top and twisted, but stopped. What was wrong? Why couldn't she keep turning it? The top wasn't stuck, but her hand refused to move it any further. She didn't want to go. Even though she'd made up her mind to go to veterinary school, her heart wasn't really excited about the prospect. Oh, she wanted to learn more about caring for and healing horses, but to do so in her time had her feeling lonely and sad.

Even surrounding herself with her beloved horses, she couldn't settle on that future. All her adult life, she'd felt something missing and it was as if she were waiting for something... no, for someone. For Peter.

She put the orb back in her pack and raced through her morning bathing ritual. Still sore but feeling alive and excited at seeing Peter again, she picked up her pack and headed to the port. Could she make it there before the ship left? She had to, she had to know Peter was safe, and even if he rejected her she would be happy in the knowledge he was on his way back to Denmark, back to his life and family.

Morning sunlight streamed down from the sky, pushing the shadows of night away in its path. As she hurried through the streets following the thickening scent of salt to the sea, a shiver of apprehension crawled up her spine.

Was she setting herself up for more heartache? Would Peter even want to see her? Even want to be with her? *Toughen up, Max.* She had to know one way or the other and even if he didn't want her to go with him, she'd at least wait until the ship cleared port and was on its way to its first stop. People like Peter weren't in history books, and if she left now, she would never know for sure that he and Karina got on that ship.

A shudder of anticipation rolled through her chest. It was somewhat exciting not knowing what would happen. Would she stay or would she have to leave, brokenhearted but content that that was the way things were already foretold in her time?

For once in her life she had no control over her future. Her heart and life were in Peter's hands, and she hoped like mad he was up for it.

The ship sounded its horn and Max picked up her pace. If she was right that was just a warning call, and everyone would now be boarding the ship. She rounded a warehouse and searched the crowd for Peter and Karina.

Spotting them, she wondered why they weren't joining the queue to climb the gangplank.

CHAPTER 23

P eter pulled Karina out of the line and searched all the entrances to the wharf.

"What are you—ah, is Maxine coming here? I thought you said goodbye already."

"We did, but now I am regretting my reason for leaving her."

Karina joined in the search for Max. "I am glad. You would have been a very sorrowful companion without her. But why should she come here? Perhaps we need to go to her."

Peter stopped looking. "You're right. I have to find her before she leaves." Dread grew in the pit of his stomach. Had she already gone back to her time? Was he too late? Why hadn't he thought to go back to her before now?

But it was only when he and Karina stood in line, ready to board the ship that would take him away from Russia, that his heart began to ache at the thought of leaving and never seeing Max again. His legs filled with lead and there was no way he could board that ship without her.

"You get on the ship and I'll get Max."

"No. I'm not leaving you. What if you don't make it back in time? I cannot take the voyage on my own."

"I thought you said you were old enough to do whatever you liked."

"I'm not old enough to sail so far on my own. What will I do when we change ships? I will not know where to go."

"I'm not arguing about it with you. Get on the ship and wait for me there."

He glanced back to the line, which had diminished so much that there were only four people at the top of the gangplank. He watched them board and pushed Karina toward the ship.

"Go."

"No. Look, it's Maxine."

Peter looked to where she pointed, and Max was standing at the corner of a building.

He called out. "Max."

Her mouth spread in a wide smile and she ran toward him. He too sprinted to her, his heart soaring with hope and happiness. His arms ached to encompass her. They were so close, only meters apart, when three thugs appeared from out of the building, one of them snatching Max's arm and pushing it behind Max's back so hard Max screamed.

The thug put a handgun to Max's temple.

Peter plied his legs as fast as he could and called to Karina over his shoulder. "Get to the ship."

He didn't wait to see if she obeyed him, instead careening into the two thugs who stood as if waiting for further instructions from their leader.

Fists and boots flew in all directions, but Peter soon knocked one then the other out. One with his fist and the other with the butt of his handgun.

"Too late, Peter."

Peter spun to the speaker, knowing instantly the voice belonged to Elena. How could he have not recognized her when she grabbed Max.

Her mouth was smiling but her eyes filled with hate as she jerked Max's arm further up her back. Max gasped as Elena spoke. "There is no White Army coming to save you this time."

Her gun clicking as she pressed it to Max's head told Peter she had taken the safety off. If he didn't do something soon, she would kill Max there and then. If he rushed her, she would shoot. If he did nothing, she would shoot.

He looked at Max. She mashed her lips together hard and used her eyes to tell him something. He couldn't read what she meant, but he knew she was going to fight back.

"Listen to me, Elena. If you shoot her like this, in cold blood, the authorities will kill you. Let her go and live your life."

"I don't care if I am killed. I don't have a life without you." She pushed the nose of the gun harder against Max's head, making her cry out in pain. "Before she came along, you and I were good together. I know you would have loved me like I loved you if we spent more time together, but she took that chance from me, from you. She has no right to live."

Max rolled her eyes to the brightening sky and quickly bending her knee, she smashed the heel of her boot so hard into Elena's knee, the sound of shattering bone had Peter instinctively taking action.

Elena screamed out in agony. Max ducked and Peter sailed over her head into Elena's chest. The gun fired and Peter felt a sting in his shoulder, but the adrenaline racing through his body had him wrenching the gun from Elena's hand and throwing it as far as he could. He pinned her to the wharf.

"You will pay for your deeds."

Karina shouted from the top of the gangplank. "Peter. Maxine. Quickly."

A constable with wharf workers in tow ran toward them. The constable blew his whistle and Peter got up and yanked Elena to her feet.

"Here." He pushed the woman at the constable and nodded to where her gun sat on the thick boards. "That's her gun." He gazed at Max.

"She's had a hard life, Peter."

He nodded and faced the constable. "Take her, and once the ship is gone you can free her." He turned and took Max's arm. "Come on, we have a ship to catch."

"Wait," the constable said. "I have to question you first."

"We haven't got time." Hoping the men before him were White sympathizers, he added, "Princess Karina is on board and I am her protection."

He and Max didn't wait to hear the constable's response and raced as fast as they could to the quickly withdrawing walkway. They hurtled up to the end and jumped onto the ship, collapsing onto the deck laughing, crying, kissing, and hugging.

"I thought I had lost you," Peter gasped.

"And I thought I'd never see you again."

He nibbled the tip of her ear. "Will you marry me?"

Max gazed up into his eyes and his heart leapt into his throat.

She held his face in her hands. "Yes, Peter, a thousand times yes."

A smile spread across his lips and he took her into his arms.

Karina clapped and bobbed on her toes. "You're to be married? I am so happy for you both, but I think you should get up now. Everyone is looking at you."

Peter looked at the crowd surrounding them and laughed. "I think we had better."

He helped Max onto her feet as Karina spoke to a uniformed chap.

"Is the captain available?"

"Only once the ship has left the port safely, Princess."

"*Nyet*, I'm no longer a princess of Russia, I am now a countess."

Max snuggled her head into Peter's shoulder. He recoiled with a gasp and Max pulled back. "What is it?" As she said the words, she was already pushing his coat away from his front and feeling his shoulder. She pulled her hand out and stared at it. "You've been shot." She tilted her head up so her words spread. "Get a doctor."

❦

IT HAD BEEN THREE DAYS OF CLEAR SAILING AND MAX WAS thankful Peter's shoulder was healing nicely with no sign of infection. While it was still sore, they found ways to cuddle and kiss without causing him pain.

Peter pulled back from one such liaison. "I have spoken to the captain."

"Why?"

"Because my shoulder is almost fully healed, and I cannot endure being alone with you any longer."

"What? You don't want to be alone with me anymore?"

"I do want to, I just want it to be as husband and wife. You still want to marry me, don't you?"

Max let out a breath of relief. She was worried there for a second. "Of course, silly."

"Good, the captain will perform the ceremony tomorrow, mid-morning."

"That soon?" She pulled the orb out of her handbag. "It's

time I sent this back so my family can come here for the wedding."

"They will come?"

"They wouldn't miss it."

Peter rubbed his chin. "Wouldn't it be slightly strange to suddenly have more people turn up on the ship?"

Max frowned. "I hadn't thought of that, but I'm guessing my cousin has so it all should be okay."

Peter raised his brows as if to say he didn't think so.

Screwing her nose up at the orb, Max turned the top, dropped the orb and moved back. "It's up to you now, Bree," she whispered.

※

MAX SAT IN THE STATEROOM PETER HAD ARRANGED FOR her and placed her coffee cup hard on the small table. She shot Karina a piercing look, unable to take her pacing any longer. "Karina."

"What?"

"You're acting more nervous than me, what's wrong?"

"I do not know. I've never been a part of a wedding before. I do not know what to do."

Max laughed. "You just stand there next to me. I give you my flowers to hold while Peter and I make our vows. What's so darn hard about that?"

"What if I drop the flowers?"

"Then you pick them up again." Max waved her to the chair opposite. "Sit down and eat something or you'll end up puking during the ceremony."

"Puking? You haven't used that word before."

"It means vomiting, being sick."

Karina sat and bit off a piece of toast. "I wouldn't want to do that, not in public, no, and we have to hurry, my hair takes a long time to do."

Max rubbed her face and wondered if she was ever that self-obsessed when she was a teenager. Abby's face appeared in her mind. Her sister yelling at her to stop being so dramatic. Max smiled. "The captain found a woman who will help us get ready."

"A woman? I hope she knows the latest hair fashion."

※

The woman, Miss Anderson, turned out to be none other than the lady's maid to the Dowager Empress Maria Fyodorovna, the mother of Nicholas the Second. Miss Anderson's fiancé had gotten her out of Russia and onto the ship. She felt bad about leaving the Dowager Empress but was overjoyed to be returning to her family in England with her fiancé and his family.

The dresses needed only a small amount of alterations and soon, Max and Karina were dressed and had new hairstyles.

Karina's pink dress that fit snugly around the waist and fell to her ankles suited her perfectly. Her long brown hair was loosely coiled at the back with tendrils of curls falling around her face.

She looked at Max and clapped her hands. "You are beautiful."

"Don't sound so surprised." Max gazed at her reflection in the wall mirror and laughed. She remembered Izzy acting astonished at Max's looks when she'd dressed as Cleopatra. She sighed. That seemed so long ago now.

She'd worn a blue gown then and somehow the dress she now wore had similar coloring. The skirt was lighter, but the bodice was the exact sapphire blue and the color suited Max's olive complexion like no other could, she was sure.

Karina peeked over Max's shoulder. "I like the way she did your hair."

Max did too. She especially like the way Miss Anderson rolled the front of her hair away from her face, which made her blue eyes stand out even more than usual. Even though Max's hair had grown quite a lot since she first arrived in Russia, she was glad Miss Anderson didn't take any scissors to it and left the remaining back tresses hanging loose.

Karina picked up her spray of pink flowers and handed Max her bouquet of different shades of blue flowers.

※

KARINA, WHO COULDN'T KEEP STILL, SHIFTED HER WEIGHT from one leg to the other. From behind, Max poked her in the back and whispered, "You'll be fine."

Clasping the bouquet of blue irises, Max wished she could let her nerves out physically like Karina, but she straightened her back and hoped no one could hear her heart thrumming against her ribs. After all, this was the first time she was to be married. She wrinkled her nose. And the last time.

A violin began playing a soft tune that sounded like it could have been a Brahms lullaby, but Karina didn't move. Max poked her in the back again. "Go."

Max followed Karina around the bulkhead and into the empty main dining room. The captain, some of his crew, all dressed in white formal suits, and some passengers she, Peter and Karina had befriended during the voyage were there, but Max's gaze settled on Peter. She inhaled a quick breath. How on earth he'd found a black suit that fitted him perfectly and made him look even more handsome than ever, she didn't know, but she liked it, she liked it a lot.

He smiled at her and heat filled her face as she smiled back.

She glanced around the room and her heart sank. She was sure her family would be there—after all, she and they had travelled back in the past to witness Abby and Izzy's weddings. She hoped the time device found its way back to the black orb.

Once she was alongside Peter, he took the bouquet and gave it to Karina. He held her hands to his chest, leaned forward and whispered, "Is something wrong?"

"I thought my family would be here."

He brought her hands to his lips and kissed her gloved knuckles. "You will see them again."

She nodded. Somewhere deep inside her, she knew Bree wouldn't leave her to stay in the past completely alone. She'd been the one to send them all back to Abby and Izzy; she would make sure they all came together one last time.

Peter squeezed her hands and she looked up.

"Are you ready to become my wife for all time?"

She grinned. "I am."

Max's brain felt like it was full of cotton candy. She heard the captain speak, but what he said never registered. She just stood there, gazing into Peter's love-filled eyes, and wondering how she got to be so lucky.

Peter took his pinkie ring off his hand and slid it onto Max's ring finger.

The captain's final words came through loud and clear.

"By the power vested in me, I now pronounce you man and wife."

Peter's lips crushed Max's mouth, and all thought of family, or anyone else for that matter, flew out of Max's head. She threw her arms around Peter's neck and kissed him back with every ounce of her being. She wanted to savor the very first kiss in their married life.

They finally pulled apart, and the clapping and cheers surrounded them.

Karina hugged Peter. "I am truly happy for you." She kissed him on the cheek and regarded him with admiration. "Peter, thank you. Thank you for not letting me do as I pleased. Thank you for saving me and thank you for caring."

"Karina, you are family and I love you as a sister. Do not thank me for doing what any brother would do for his sister."

She smiled. "Just know I will not forget." She turned to Max. "Maxine, thank you for everything."

Max hugged her. "You don't have to thank me either. If it wasn't for you, I would never have met Peter and I would never have been as happy as I am now."

Then it was a whirl of handshakes and good wishes from everyone there.

Miss Anderson held Max's hands. "It fills my heart with joy to see such happiness in such times of sorrow."

Max smiled.

"I do hope you will visit me while you are in London. My brother, Alfred Anderson, has opened his home to me and loves company."

"Your brother is Alfred Anderson?" Max said, unable to keep the awe from her tone. His plays were still being staged in Max's time period.

"You know my brother?"

"No, not personally, but I have heard of him and—"

Peter squeezed her to stop her saying something she would regret. "He is known on the continent as an imaginative playwright."

"Yes, of course," Miss Anderson said. "I forget his work is well known sometimes. To me, he's my little brother."

By the time Peter and Max got back together, the staff were bringing out trays of food and placing them on the tables.

Peter put an arm around Max's waist and pulled her in

close to his side. "We will have a much grander wedding once we get home."

Max shook her head. "I don't want a bigger wedding. This one was perfect, and I will remember it all the days of my life."

"So be it." And with that, he swung her around into his arms and kissed her like his very life depended on it.

EPILOGUE

A whole year later, Max sat in the courtyard sipping coffee and gazing at the mountains surrounding her and Peter's chateau. The sky's azure blue had her thinking of her wedding day. She sighed. So much had happened since then. She had met Peter's family, who were surprised to meet his wife. His mother, an intelligent woman, was immediately suspicious of Max.

She had spent many years in the United States, and she questioned Max endlessly. Finally, Peter could take no more and told her and his father the truth. They of course didn't believe it at first, but with Max's strange ways and knowledge, they finally came around.

Karina helped there—she was forthright, and they trusted her word.

"Maxine."

Peter's voice brought her out of her reverie, and his kiss on the back of her neck had her tingling from head to foot. She put her cup down on the small table and she smiled as she turned her head. He wasn't alone.

"Ilya!"

Max leapt to her feet. She wasn't sure if she should hug him, but her arms were around his neck without her consciously moving them. "How did you get here? Are you well? Is something wrong?"

He laughed and giving her a final squeeze, said, "*Nyet*. It is good to see you, Maxine."

She gazed at Peter. "Did you know he was coming? Why didn't you tell me?" She took Ilya's hands. "Are you alone?"

"Yes, this time. My wife is full of baby and could not make the voyage, but she will next time."

"Next time? You're going to visit again?"

"If you will have us, yes."

"You are always welcome here, isn't he, Peter?" Max grinned at Ilya. "It's all right, he knows everything."

"I expected that."

"Wait, a year ago, you said you were going to see Mom and Dad again. Did you see them?"

He nodded. "That is why I am here. They asked me to... how did they put it? Check on you."

Max laughed. "That'd be right."

Max loved hearing about them, but a sadness filled her being and her smile faded.

Peter put his arm around her waist. "Do not be sad, my love. They are alive and well in this time."

"Peter is right," Ilya said. "Come, let us talk."

They sat at the small table, drank coffee, ate sweet Danish pastries and talked about her parents and what happened in Russia after they left until midday.

Ilya got to his feet. "It is time."

Max and Peter stood up also. "Time for what?" Max asked.

"Your anniversary surprise," Peter said.

"You remembered."

He scooped her up into his arms and his breath whispered

against her lips as he said, "How could I forget the first day of the rest of my life with my beloved wife?"

He enclosed her mouth with his and her entire body answered in her kiss. The world around them vanished in that moment, and Max pressed in closer.

Someone clearing their throat bought Max to her senses, and she finished the kiss with a quick peck before turning to Ilya. She tried to look contrite. "Sorry."

Peter grinned at Max. "I'm not, but we should look after our guest now and continue with our private conversation at a later time."

Max nodded and picked up her bag. "I forgot." She pulled out a small box and handed it to Peter. "Happy anniversary."

He opened it and she added, "I never had a wedding ring to give you when we married. I hope you like it."

Peter gave her a love-filled look that made her heart flip and put the ring on.

"Thank you, my love. I will never take it off." He glanced at Ilya, who was giving him a hard stare. "But quickly now. We must go."

He took Max's hand and guided her to the large reception room in the center of the chateau. Resting his hand on the brass doorknobs, he said, "Are you ready?"

Max couldn't guess for the life of her what could be behind the thick wooden doors. What could be so big, he couldn't bring it to her in the courtyard?

Excitement welled in her chest and she nodded.

He flung the door wide and voices shouted. "Surprise!"

Max gaped at her family. Everybody was there, Abby and Iain, Izzy and Edward, and Garrett, but no Bree. Abby embraced Max first. "It is so good to see you."

Izzy bounced on the balls of her feet. "That's enough, Abs. My turn."

Abby moved to the side and Izzy covered Max in hugs and kisses. "I thought I'd never see you again."

Max laughed. "I can't believe you're here." She held out her arms to Garrett. "Come here, little brother."

He did, and Max was sure he held her longer than he'd ever held her before.

"Sorry we missed your wedding."

Max looked from one sibling to the other. "I have to admit, I sort of thought you would be there."

"We would have been if our contact was, but Ilya was still deep in Russia," Garrett said. "And somehow Bree knew you weren't."

Max frowned. It seemed Bree only shared as much as she needed to. "How did she know?"

Garrett shrugged. "She uses the black orb somehow. Don't ask because whenever I question her, she just says it's her job to do what is right, not explain every little thing to us."

"It doesn't matter," Izzy said. "We're here now, and shouldn't you be introducing your husband to us?"

Max introduced Peter to each one. Izzy hugged him. "I knew Max would find love sooner or later."

Peter put his arm around Max and drew her into his side. "I am glad it was me she found."

Edward moved alongside his wife. "I am Elizabeth's husband, Edward." He held out his hand and bent his head in a small bow. "Count."

Peter shook his hand and gave him a one-armed hug. "I have heard much about you, my lord."

Abby gave Peter a quick hug. "Welcome to the family." She waved a hand at Iain. "And this is Laird Iain Maclaren, my husband."

Iain gave Peter a wide smile. "One thing I will tell you, Peter. You will never be bored."

Peter laughed. "I believe you."

Karina stood by the sidewall, wiping tears from her eyes. Max rushed to her side. "What's wrong?"

"Nothing, these are happy tears. I am so glad you have your family. I like them all."

"They are your family too," Max said.

Karina beamed at her and seemed to take a new look at her newly increased family members.

"Karina's been filling us in on what's been happening to you," Garrett said, pulling a camera out of his pocket. "Smile."

They did and he took the shot.

The rest of the afternoon flew by with much laughter, talking and teasing. Max couldn't remember enjoying herself so much, but her gaze always seemed to land on Garrett as he roamed around the room taking photographs. She couldn't help but wonder what Bree had in mind for him. The more she thought about it, the more she suspected her cousin had planned everything from the moment she arrived at the Davis family home.

First Abby found her beloved, Iain, on a bleak Scottish moor of all places, then Izzy met the man of her dreams when his carriage nearly ran her over. Max looked at Peter. He, Ilya, Edward and Iain were getting along famously. She smiled and silently thanked her cousin for helping her to meet her very own once in a lifetime love.

Peter strolled up to Max and wrapped his arms around her. "Are you happy?"

"This is the best surprise ever. Thank you."

He snuggled her neck and whispered in her ear. "I love you, Maxine."

She leant back and pierced him with an intent gaze. "I love you, more and more every day."

Thank you so much for reading *From Cafés to Cossacks*!

Book IV in The Time Orb Series, *From Studios to Saloons*, is available at your preferred store now.

And... if you would like to learn about new releases in the series *and* have the chance to grab *Henrietta's Dance*, a Regency Romance Novella, please head over to my website and join my newsletter.

https://callieberkham.com/

I value our friendship and will never share your email, ever. And don't worry if you have already joined my mailing list because all the free books will be added to my newsletter as I write them.

More books by Callie
The Time Orb Series:

From Suits to Kilts
From Bars to Ballrooms
From Cafés to Cossacks
From Studios to Saloons

Visit my website for the latest news: www.callieberkham.com

Printed in Great Britain
by Amazon